Francis King, drama critic of the *Sunday Telegraph*, is a former winner of the Somerset Maugham Prize, and of the *Yorkshire Post* Novel of the Year award. He reviews fiction, notably for the *Spectator*, and non-fiction, and was for some years President of International PEN. He wrote his first three novels when he was still an undergraduate at Oxford. He then joined the British Council and travelled extensively. He now devotes himself entirely to writing. Francis King lives in West London.

'Francis King, one of the finest contemporary novelists, is prolific, fluent, witty and moving . . . he is a master novelist.'

MELVYN BRAGG, *Punch*

'Francis King's writing is always accomplished and elegant.'

A. S. BYATT, *The Times*

'Francis King writes with beautiful subtlety.'

ELIZABETH BERRIDGE, *Daily Telegraph*

'Nobody is better than Francis King at handling loving but uncertain relationships, and at illuminating the spaces between people. He is as tireless as a great scientist in his determination to get at the truth of how we feel. No one is more aware of the contradictions we contain, and he reveals them exquisitely.'

ALLAN MASSIE, *Scotsman*

PUNISHMENTS

'Has the subtlety and psychological acumen we expect from Francis King . . . the book finely details the confrontation between the English and the Germans.'

Observer

'This short novel is so simple to read, and so unsettling to have read. Its permanent legacy should be terror not only of war but all moral complacency.'

VICTORIA GLENDINNING, *The Times*

Francis King

PUNISHMENTS

FLAMINGO
Published by Fontana Paperbacks

First published in Great Britain
by Hamish Hamilton Ltd 1989

First published in Flamingo
in 1990 by Fontana Paperbacks

Flamingo is an imprint of Fontana Paperbacks,
part of the Collins Publishing Group,
8 Grafton Street, London W1X 3LA

Copyright © 1989 by Francis King

Printed and bound in Great Britain by
William Collins Sons & Co. Ltd, Glasgow

CONTENTS

1981

If the ramshackle bus had a driver, I didn't see him. Stinking of petrol fumes and the acrid smoke of black-market cigarettes, it bucked and lurched down a long, straight road. The road, pitted with bomb-craters inadequately packed with soil and rubble, bisected a landscape eerie in its total lack of trees. Jürgen and I were alone, sitting side by side on the hard, dusty seat at the rear, his left hand gripping my right.

'Is Rosenheim beautiful?'

'Yes, of course. It's one of the most beautiful towns in Germany. Even more beautiful than Hildingen.'

But in my dream I already knew, as I hadn't known those thirty-three years ago, the truth about Rosenheim, so that I cried out in mingled rage and anguish: 'Why do you have to tell me these lies?'

Jürgen laughed. 'A joke. A joke! Where is the famous English sense of humour?'

It is then that I awake, to yet another dawn of this long, hot summer, as the birds begin to twitter in the sycamore at the far end of the garden, and a breeze through the wide-open window plucks at the sheet thrown back from my naked body. Beside me, an arm trailing over the bed and the sheet drawn up to her chin, Sally sleeps on. I feel a sudden resentment against her, sunk in an oblivion denied to me.

In the pearly light of not yet six o'clock, I walk down the narrow garden, the dew on the uncut grass – yes, yes, Sally, this evening or tomorrow evening I'll cut it – making my slippers soggy. I place myself in one of the

3

garden chairs and rest an arm along the chill metal top of the table beside it. I listen to the racket of the birds, as I think again of that dream. Having dreamed less and less of Jürgen through all these years, why do I now, this summer, so often dream of him? There is a rustle in the herbaceous border and then, with a plaintive squawk – but it only sounds plaintive, really she's overjoyed to see me – Princess, my Siamese, *our* Siamese, Sally's and my Siamese, leaps into my lap. She presses herself against me, her purr as loud as the racket of the birds – which, of course, she's been stalking. I stroke her, then I tug at the burrs in her coat. Docilely, she allows me to tug and tug again. Perhaps, since she goes on purring, she even enjoys the tugging.

Now it is no longer that dream of a journey I recall, but the reality of another journey. The start of a journey into a knowledge of others – and, more important, into a knowledge of myself? Yes, one could call it that. Indeed, that is how I myself have often called it, exclaiming to myself, 'Oh, how innocent I was!' At eighteen, in the immediate aftermath of the war, it was possible to be so innocent. Such innocence was impossible for my children. It will be even more impossible for my grandchildren. Infant hands reach out for the forbidden fruit. Milk-teeth, small, sharp and greedy, close on it. I had no idea of what was happening and Sally had even less. When at last we bit into the flesh, it was like that of some sleepy pear, soft, flavourless, vaguely nauseating. We might have been biting into a ball of wool.

1948

I

There was the leaden sky and there was the flat, inter-minable plain with its ruined houses and factories and its fractured trees and stunted bushes, all looking as though they'd been drawn in smudged sepia with a clumsy brush. The train halted, it was shunted back and forth into sidings, it chugged on for a while. At first the eleven of us, crowded into a carriage for eight – a girl sat on a boy's lap until, impatiently, he pushed her off, another boy crouched on the floor, hands clasped round knees – had chatted excitedly. Then, one by one, we'd all fallen silent, reading books, or dozing, or going out into the corridor to stand gazing in melancholy awe at the people-less desolation.

A Cambridge undergraduate called Harry, sturdily handsome despite the acne that had pitted his cheeks and the back of his neck as though with shrapnel, suddenly jerked down the window, leaned far out and vomited. With a combination of distaste and curiosity, I watched his shoulders heaving, his fingers whitening on the sill as he gripped it tightly. Then he turned back into the carriage, raised the window once more, and drew a crum-pled ball of handkerchief out of his no less crumpled flannels. Saliva glistened on his chin. 'Christ! I feel better for that. To think that my father commanded a corvette and a train makes me sick!' No one said anything. He grunted, sighed and squeezed himself back between his girl-friend, Jessica, and another boy from Cambridge. Jessica put a hand on his knee, a gesture of sympathy, protection, perhaps even love.

I wondered if it was indeed the train that had made him sick or one of the thick sandwiches that we'd been given at the Hook for the journey, some made of Spam and some of eggs the yolks of which had a greenish tinge, similar to that of the leaden sky under which we were now crawling. I glanced sideways at Mervyn. He looked so clean, neat and composed, in his white shirt and brown woollen tie, his carefully pressed flannels, his dark-green Harris tweed sports jacket and his suede shoes. He also looked so young, like a precocious schoolboy, that it was difficult to believe that, three years before, he'd won a DSO for gallantry at Anzio. 'What are you reading?' I'd asked him on board the bucking ship, to receive the smiling answer, 'Nothing you'd understand.' Later, when he'd gone below to the lavatory, I'd picked up the book from his deckchair and found it to be the *Oxford Book of Greek Verse*. Well, yes, I knew no Greek, since even as a child I'd wanted to be a doctor. But why that contempt? After all, I didn't despise him for his ignorance of biology or anatomy.

Sally was crushed against my other side. But I have no memory of her – how she looked, what she was doing. Mervyn, though five years my senior, was then my closest friend. Sally was also a friend. But if anyone had, at that moment, told me that eventually I'd marry her, I'd have burst into embarrassed, incredulous laughter. Like all women then, she was for me vaguely seductive, vaguely mysterious, vaguely disturbing.

... I slept. When I awoke, the train had once again halted and Harry was in the corridor, this time opening not the window but the door. I assumed he was again going to be sick. Then I saw that, in joke, he was pretending to get out of the train and that Jessica, clutching hold of his baggy trousers by the seat, was pulling him back. Both of them were laughing. 'But I must have a

8

drink, must, must, must!' he was protesting. At the top of an otherwise bare hill, I could see the bombed remains of a building, with '*Bierkeller*' written across it on a board that had slipped from horizontal to diagonal. 'Idiot!' Jessica cried out. 'Oh, idiot!' He turned round to her now, putting hands on either side of her cheeks, preparatory to kissing her. But she gave him a shove away from her.

I watched them closely. My female relatives apart, I'd never kissed a woman.

Again I slept.

The next time I awoke, it was to rub a hand over the grime obscuring the window beside me. I could taste that same grime, metallic and thick, on my tongue and at the back of my throat. Yet again I peered out at the grey, grim landscape from the stationary train. Then I said: 'How hideous it is. One thought that what they'd suffered from the raids was no worse than what we suffered.'

Mervyn lowered his book on to his knees, leaned forward and gazed at me ruminatively. 'Did one?'

'Well, I did.'

'Then you're in for a lot of surprises.'

Sally stirred. Then she said in her soft, drawling voice, 'I think that I came here to be surprised. I want surprises.'

II

Mervyn's tone was vaguely puzzled, as though he'd just made the discovery of something that he should have known long before. 'I don't mind discomfort. But I do hate a lack of privacy.'

It was our first morning in Hildingen, and the three of us sat at a grease-smeared table, gulping coffee – 'Made from acorns, of course,' Mervyn had grumbled – and tearing voraciously with our teeth at rolls stuffed with pork luncheon meat of the consistency of rubber.

'Oh, I was so tired I hardly noticed all the people around me,' Sally said. On our arrival the sexes had been separated, each of us to lay out a sleeping bag on a hard truckle bed in the dormitories, one for girls and one for boys, to which a hard-faced, sharp-voiced ATS officer had conducted us.

'And I was so tired that I just couldn't sleep. It was as though a dog were chasing its tail round and round and round in my brain.'

'Poor Mervyn.' Briefly Sally put a hand over his. That was a period when everyone, except Mervyn himself, thought of Sally as Mervyn's girl.

'That man from King's – Henry, Harry – vomited again. Twice. Into his po. He couldn't even be bothered to go along to the bog. Disgusting! But come the morning, he was as hearty as ever. Singing while he shaved!'

'Singing?' Sally gave her loud, clear laugh, so unlike her soft, veiled voice. In those days she still had a Yorkshire accent, which cruelly Mervyn would take off. 'I thought

I heard "*Funiculi, funicula*" coming down the passage as I was waiting for a shower.'

'Hideously out of tune.'

I knew how much Mervyn, with his perfect sense of pitch, must have suffered from that out-of-tune singing. That it was out-of-tune I myself hadn't realised.

Sally tipped back her head, to drain the dregs of coffee in her thick, white cup. 'What's this morning's programme then? Has either of you any idea? If they tell us one thing, they tell us something different a few minutes later.' All her life Sally has wanted to work to a programme. She hates my kind of carefree improvisation.

Mervyn wriggled in his chair. 'Well, what I gather is that that cocky little man who met us last night – Major or was it Colonel Thwaites? – will come by to fetch us. And then we'll walk over to the university Aula. And then we'll be put on offer, like slaves. *Non angeli, sed Angli.*'

'On offer? What on earth do you mean!' I asked.

Mervyn explained irritably, as though it were only stupidity that had prevented Sally and me from knowing about it already. The German students taking part in this Anglo-German summer school had been asked to put up the English visitors in their homes or their lodgings. There probably wouldn't be enough places for all the English, and those not invited would continue to stay in the dormitories. 'One really doesn't know whether one would rather be chosen or remain here,' Mervyn concluded. 'Neither prospect seems particularly enticing, does it?'

Not for the first time, I wondered why he'd joined our party. Could it have been in order to spend the summer vac with Sally even though she seemed so often to irritate or bore him? Or had he felt drawn, against his will, to this race to which he so often referred as Krauts or Huns – admittedly putting each of those pejoratives into ironic inverted commas, so that they seemed to express contempt as much for the sort of people who habitually used them as for those to whom they were applied?

He stooped, opened the rucksack at his feet and pulled out from it what looked like a substantial school exercise book. He opened the book on a corner of the table, as far away from us as possible, and then took a fountain-pen from the inside pocket of his jacket.

'Your diary?' I asked, knowing already that it was.

'My diary. I must remember to record every horror in it. Like putting amputated toes and fingers into a jar of formaldehyde.'

'I wish I could read it,' Sally said.

'Not a chance. Don't you dare!'

'Perhaps I should keep a diary too.'

He shook his head. 'You haven't got it in you.'

'What haven't I got in me?'

'Well, for one thing, the persistence.'

With a smile, Sally nodded, pleased, rather than offended, by the verdict.

III

Small, pink-faced, wide-bottomed, a swagger stick under an arm, Colonel Thwaites barked out his instructions, like a drill instructor, before leading us off to the Aula. Then he trotted over to attach himself to me as we descended a narrow alley. This attention did not embarrass me, it did not even strike me as odd. At that period, with my regular features, my wavy black hair, and my slender but athletic build, I was used to being noticed. In fact, it annoyed me if I was not. In my quiet, self-effacing way, I was vain, terribly vain.

'So what d'you make of Hildingen?'

'Arriving here was rather like waking from a nightmare.'

'I'd have thought it was more like entering one.' As Thwaites looked across at me, I noticed, with distaste, that nicotine had given his straggly moustache the yellow-brown tints of an autumn leaf.

'I mean, the war might never have taken place to judge from Hildingen. But that journey – horrific.' Where the hell were Mervyn and Sally? Why had they abandoned me to this ghastly little man?

'Yes, they were lucky here – bloody lucky, with the luck of the devil. And now we're lucky – to be here instead of in some outsize bomb-crater like Hanover. This is one of the great universities of the world, you know. Famous for its physics.' I hadn't known. 'Heine said the two things he'd always remember about Hildingen were the excellence of its sausages and the ugliness of its women.

Nothing about the physics of course. He was rusticated from here.'

Still wondering what had happened to the other two, I'd been repeatedly looking over my shoulder. Now I said: 'You're not a regular soldier, are you?'

'Good God, no. Schoolmaster. That's why I was chucked into the education corps and not into something more exciting.'

'And dangerous.' If that sounded snide, I'd wanted it to do so. Thwaites blushed. Then, a moment later, with some inaudible excuse, he trotted off to join a group of three girls ahead of us.

In the assembly hall, Mervyn suddenly materialised, to stand close to me, as though for our mutual protection. 'Did I say a slave market? I should have said a marriage market.'

The Germans were self-consciously ranged around the walls, while we English stood even more self-consciously huddled in the middle, sipping at the cups of weak tea or bitter coffee handed to us on our entry and, in many cases, also puffing at the cigarettes that we'd been able to buy at the Naafi at the Hook.

'Give me a fag.' Mervyn didn't usually smoke.

'I haven't got one. I'm giving up. I told you.'

'Oh, blast! . . . Sally? Have you got a fag?' She'd now appeared beside us.

That was when I'd first seen Jürgen, becoming aware that a handsome German, in open-necked shirt and extraordinarily short shorts that revealed extraordinarily long, muscular legs, was pushing his way through the crowds in our direction. When he reached us, he was smiling with none of the nervous wariness of his fellow students as they approached their future guests. 'Excuse me.' It was Mervyn on whom his eyes had been fixed while crossing the room, and it was to Mervyn that he now gave a little

14

bow and held out his hand. 'Jürgen Koesten.' It was only after he had greeted Sally in similar fashion that, as though as an afterthought, he turned at last to me.

'Your name, please?' he demanded, as our hands touched. Then, when I told him, he repeated it twice, 'Michael Gregg, Michael Gregg,' as though incredulous that anyone could be called anything so absurd. Mervyn and Sally had already mumbled their names, as though ashamed of them, when they had shaken hands.

At that, as though he had no further interest in me, Jürgen turned back to Mervyn. 'Would you like to stay with me? We must share a bedroom, but the bedroom is big. But not very comfortable,' he added with a smile.

'Well . . . that's very kind of you . . . ' Mervyn sounded reluctant, ungracious. As so often on such occasions, I felt ashamed for him. I also felt angry that he should have received an invitation that I had expected to be mine. Would I, uninvited by any of the German students, have to continue to stay in that doss-house of a hostel?

'Your friend – Michael,' – he did not even look at me as he said this – 'can also stay in my house if he wishes. But I am afraid that Sally cannot do so. Men students must stay with men students, women students with women students. Never mind. Sally' – he smiled at her with sudden warmth – 'can stay with Jutta. You will like Jutta, Sally. Now I will call her.'

Jürgen turned and shouted, 'Jutta, Jutta, Jutta!' Then he stood on tiptoe and waved an arm back and forth in the air. Eventually a girl, leaning against the wall, straightened and waved back. With her diminutive stature, her flat chest and her short-cut reddish-brown hair, she looked, at that distance, like a child of nine or ten. Then, as she walked towards us, I noticed the network of lines under pale blue eyes with a curious milkish tinge to them. Two teeth were missing from a corner of her mouth, so that when she smiled – as she did now – it was almost a grimace.

Jürgen introduced us, and Jutta then shook our hands. Although, as we soon learned, she was a student of English literature, her accent wasn't nearly as good as his.

'Shall we go first to my house?' Jürgen suggested. 'Then we can go on to Jutta's. She lives quite near to me.'

Colonel Thwaites had instructed us to carry our luggage over with us from the hostel, and then to stack it in a passage outside the hall. Now Jürgen insisted on carrying not only Sally's but also Mervyn's suitcase. Why I wondered, with a sense of humiliation, should Mervyn have been given this favoured treatment? Jutta had already shouldered Sally's pack, refusing to relinquish it when, with typical independence, Sally had protested that she could easily manage it herself. Mervyn made no effort to wrest his suitcase from Jürgen. He seemed to accept that the German should act as his beast of burden.

Jürgen, carrying the two suitcases as though they were no more weighty than shopping bags, led the way jauntily down a cobbled street which descended, in a series of precipitate drops, beside the hall. At that time and in that place, we must have seemed a strange quintet. A number of people gave us surreptitious glances. Then, blatant in his curiosity, a shabby old man, his huge nose inflamed, stopped, leaned on his stick, and stared at us, turning his head to do so as we passed. Gaily, Jürgen called out something to him in German, and then he and Jutta laughed. After an uncertain pause, the old man joined in their laughter. Mervyn then also said something to the old man.

Jutta stopped in her tracks, the weight of the rucksack making her head tilt forward. 'But you speak German! You speak German well!'

Mervyn smiled and shrugged. 'Oh, I've picked up just a little.'

'You are too modest,' Jutta said, as though, after lengthy deliberation, she were making a serious reflection on his character.

We now took a path – a short cut, Jürgen told us – running behind a row of gloomy houses set in gardens overgrown with weeds and brambles. In many of the gardens, washing swayed back and forth in the breeze. Jutta began to ask me questions about myself – how old was I? how old were my parents? did I have any sisters? did I have any brothers? – while the other three, Jürgen in the middle, walked on ahead of us in silence.

At one moment I broke off my conversation with Jutta, to call out: 'Mervyn, don't you think you should take one of the suitcases and give Jürgen a rest?' Mervyn then made a half-hearted effort to do so, abandoned as soon as Jürgen assured him: 'No, no! They are not heavy. I am strong.'

'Yes, he is strong,' Jutta said. Her admiring tone made me wonder if she were Jürgen's girl-friend.

Soon we had reached the river, glinting wanly in the sunshine. There was sweat along Jürgen's upper lip, and dark patches under the arms of Jutta's cotton dress. But in spite of the sunlight, our brisk pace and the weight of my suitcase, I myself felt chilled. Tiredness, I decided.

On the other side of the river, across a rickety wooden bridge, we reached our destination. 'My house,' said Jürgen by the open gate, setting down the suitcases and flexing his fingers. I gazed up the drive at a large house, constructed of wood in dire need of painting, with two steep, narrow gables and shutters to the upper windows. Beside it, there was a dilapidated brick garage, with a room under a gable even steeper and narrower than that of the house. I was to come to know that room well.

An Alsatian bitch, her eyes dim, limped round the corner, as we were walking up the drive. She sniffed at Sally's hand. Always nervous of dogs – once, when she was only three, one had bitten her – Sally shrank a little until Jürgen told her: 'Don't be afraid. Once she was very fierce, she even bit people she did not like. But now she is old. She harms no one.' Sally raised the hand at which the dog had been sniffing and caressed her greying head. They stood there together, girl and dog, briefly frozen. I remember thinking how beautiful Sally looked at that moment, in a sturdily monumental way.

Jürgen opened the unlocked front-door. He called out in German but no one answered. 'The house is empty.'

'For once it is empty,' Jutta said.

The hall would have been dark even if it hadn't been crammed with so much heavy furniture and so many thickly varnished pictures – of men in high collars ramrod-stiff at desks or in breeches ramrod-stiff on horses, of high-coiffured women languishing in rooms as overfurnished as this hall, of children posed in self-conscious groups, some standing, some seated and some squatting. Jürgen put down the suitcases. Then Mervyn removed his rucksack from his narrow shoulders and, with a sigh, put that down too. I said to Jutta: 'Let me help you off with that.' But already Jutta had swung down Sally's rucksack on to the black-and-white tiled floor. Like Jürgen, she was clearly tough. Her childlike body was tensile and wiry.

Jürgen led us into a sitting-room crammed, like the hall, with lustrous, heavy Biedermeier furniture and thickly varnished pictures, their elaborate gold frames glinting out of the general murk. 'I will make you some coffee,' he said, when we were seated.

Mervyn was giving everything around him sharply darting glances. I knew that he was asking himself:

18

What's it going to be like living here for a fortnight? Is it going to be hell? He was expecting the worst. He always did.

We sat waiting for Jürgen, who'd gone off to make the coffee, refusing Jutta's insistent offers to make it herself. 'Nice house,' Jutta said, sitting forward on the edge of an upright chair and licking her lips nervously, as she gazed, head tilted, at a late nineteenth-century picture of a girl in a red jacket, her hands in a muff, with a large, tousled dog lying at her feet. 'Very nice. Where I live ...' She looked over to Sally and, having caught her eye, then smiled and shrugged. 'Sorry, Sally. Not like this, not at all.'

'I'm sure everything will be fine. In any case, I'm not in the least fussy. The two boys are the fussy ones.' As so often, Sally, her knees and ankles close together and her hands in her lap, gave an impression of easygoing calm.

'I'm not in the least fussy!' I protested.

Mervyn laughed, leaning back in his armchair and stretching his legs out before him. 'One must have some standards. That's what Sally has never grasped.'

Jutta looked at him, puzzled. Then she got up and crossed over to a framed certificate on a wall. Head on one side, her lips slightly moving, she began to read it like the child she so much resembled. I wondered what the certificate said.

Mervyn now also got up and went over to a table. He picked up a book that was lying open, face downwards, on it. 'Conrad! Well, fancy that! *Under Western Eyes*. Far greater than any novel Dostoievsky ever wrote.'

'Oh, you don't really believe that!' Sally protested, rising, as so often, to his bait.

He smiled mischievously. 'I'm not sure if I do or don't. I must think about it.'

19

Jürgen brought in the coffee on a tray covered with an embroidered, lace-fringed cloth. The clumsily ornate cups were encrusted with emerald leaves. The coffee was in a tarnished silver pot, ivory inset into its handle. There were some almond-paste biscuits on a silver plate with a dark-blue glass liner.

'You shouldn't have gone to all this trouble,' I said. At a briefing session back in London, we'd been warned that in Germany coffee and food were both still scarce.

Mervyn, uninvited, put out a narrow hand, took one of the biscuits off the plate, and popped it in his mouth. Jürgen smiled at the action, as one might in indulgence for a naughty child. Jutta was again perched on the edge of her chair, hands under thighs. Hesitantly she shook her head, her bell of short-cut reddish-brown hair swaying from side to side, when Jürgen held out the plate of biscuits to her. Had he insisted, I knew that she'd have taken one. Sally and I also shook our heads.

From the hall there came a dry, persistent coughing, followed by the tap-tap-tap of a stick striking the tiled floor. The door creaked open and an old man, in morning coat and wing collar, pince-nez on a ribbon round his scrawny neck, slowly limped in. Jürgen and Jutta jumped to their feet, to be followed by Sally and me and then, reluctantly, by Mervyn.

Jürgen spoke to the old man in German, addressing him as 'Papa'. Then he said in English: 'This is my father.'

'So he lives here too,' I said, as I stepped forward to take the blue, bony hand extended first to me. I had supposed the house to be merely Jürgen's lodgings.

'Of course! This house belongs to him,' Jutta said.

The introductions over, Jürgen said something to the old man, pointing to an armchair. The old man shook his head. Jürgen then turned to Mervyn: 'My father is a professor at the university. He is a geneticist.'

The old man passed a trembling hand, a thick gold band on the wedding-finger, through his close-cropped white hair. The vaguely troubled look that there had been in his red-rimmed eyes now dissipated. They lit up with friendliness. In English he said: 'Please! Please do not stand for me! I came here merely to get something.' He stooped and picked up the copy of *Under Western Eyes*. Then, motionless, he stared at me, his eyes still alight with friendliness.

Embarrassed, I felt I had to say something. 'You speak English even better than your son.'

The old man shrugged, the book now under an arm. 'Once I spoke it well. You know, I had an English tutor – just as Jürgen had an English nurse. We loved the English.' Was there any significance in the past tense? 'Also I spent a year at Cambridge. But now ... So many years have passed ... No practice ...'

He wandered out through the door, leaving it open behind him.

'What a sweet old man!' Sally exclaimed. Throughout our conversation she had been watching him with eager, bright eyes.

Jutta nodded her approval of this verdict. 'Also a great man,' she said firmly.

Later, as we were finishing our coffee, Jürgen turned to Mervyn: 'I am sorry that it is impossible to give you a room to yourself. I am sorry that you must share with me and my cousin Heinz. Accommodation is very difficult in Hildingen now. Your people have – how do you say? – commandeered many houses, and there are many, many refugees, like Jutta, from the East. So we have many people living in this house. My father's assistant from the university, my two aunts, my cousin, two other people. I am sorry.' Then, as an apparent afterthought, he turned to me. 'I am also sorry, Michael' – he hesitated before my name, as though he had difficulty in remembering it – 'that you must sleep in the little room above the garage. We do not use it in the winter, it is too cold. I am afraid that we have stored things there. What are we to do? So many people, so little room.'

'Oh, it doesn't matter!' But I felt piqued that I should have been relegated to what was all too clearly a lumber-room outside the main house. 'It's a situation we knew about already. We've the same kind of problem in Oxford – though not so bad. In the old days the under-graduates would each have a set of rooms – a bedroom and a sitting-room. Now they have to muck in together.'

'Muck in?' Jürgen savoured the phrase. Then he said: 'I know the word "muck". I like that "muck in". Yes, I like that. Good.'

Mervyn, who'd once again been gazing around the room suddenly asked, 'Who plays the piano?' A Steinway grand stood in a dark corner, a Spanish shawl draped across it.

'No one now. My mother used to play it. She is – no longer here.' Did he mean that she was dead? I didn't dare to ask.

'Do you play, Mervyn?'

Mervyn shrugged and pulled down the corners of his mouth. 'A little.'

'He plays beautifully,' Sally said. At that period, she was full of admiration for him. 'He could be a pro-fessional if he wanted to.'

'Sally always exaggerates. You'll soon learn that about her.'

'This evening you must play to us,' Jürgen said.

'Oh, Christ, no!'

When the time came for the two girls to leave, Jutta manfully heaved up Sally's suitcase. 'Oh, let me take that!' Sally protested, also grasping the handle. On an impulse I offered: 'Shall I come with you to carry the suitcase?'

Jutta cried out: 'No, no! It is nothing! I am used to carrying. I am strong.'

But, feeling excluded by Jürgen, I felt the need to make an ally of the German girl. I persisted, until with a cross little laugh Jutta agreed: 'Very well, Michael!'

'You'll never find your way back,' Mervyn warned.

'Of course I shall.'

I've always prided myself on my sense of direction.

The three of us walked down the drive, with the Alsatian trailing behind. At the gate Jutta turned and shouted at the dog in German, presumably telling her to go back, but still she followed us, her coat dull in the now brilliant sunshine. Again Jutta turned. This time she not merely shouted but stamped a small foot. The dog slunk away.

'You and Mervyn are lucky to stay with Jürgen. Even above the garage. The house is good. He will look after you well.' She was staggering along, a little ahead of me, her shoulders sagging under the weight of Sally's pack, which she had refused to cede to her. 'Yes, you are lucky,' she went on. 'Where I stay – where Sally will stay – is not so good.'

Four long, low brick buildings made a rectangle hemming in an uneven expanse of yellowing grass. Washing fluttered from a line strung between two trees, as it had fluttered in so many of the gardens that we'd passed earlier. Was there a universal washing-day in Hildingen or even in the whole of Germany? Under the washing, a girl, in a one-piece, dark-blue bathing costume, lay out on a blanket. Her eyes were closed, her arms outstretched. At the sound of our feet on the gravel of the path, she first opened her eyes wide and then stared not at the girls but at me. She said nothing to Jutta, and

Jutta said nothing to her, although presumably they were fellow residents. Her obvious interest in me gave a brief upward jerk to my drooping morale.

Inside the building towards which Jutta had walked with a quickening of pace, the hall and corridor were both of raw concrete. The walls were of the same raw concrete, bare except for a notice-board, with tattered notices fluttering on it as they were snatched at by the breeze from an open window.

Jutta opened a door. She laughed, with a strange note of hysteria in her laughter. 'Like a prison,' she said. 'Like' – she groped for a word – 'like a cell, yes?'

There were two narrow beds, each with a single pillow and what appeared to be a khaki army blanket, and each with a locker, painted a sickly green, at its foot. The door of the single wardrobe hung ajar, to reveal some dresses. There was an old-fashioned washhand-stand, with basin, ewer and slop-pail. There was a blind but no curtains.

I hoisted the suitcase on to one of the lockers. Jutta wriggled out of the straps of the pack and placed it on the other. She rubbed at a shoulder. 'Welcome. Welcome to my cell.' Suddenly she sounded bitter, even hostile.

'Fine.' Sally looked around her, smiling. 'Fine,' she repeated, clearly to convince herself as much as Jutta.

'Now you will wish to unpack.' All at once she was looking totally exhausted, the network of lines suddenly deeper and darker under the milkily blue eyes.

'Right!' Sally said, making no attempt to do so.

I sank into the only chair, a wicker one, which creaked beneath me. I gazed at the two girls turn and turn about.

'For you,' Jutta said, pointing to one of the lockers. 'For you,' she said again, pointing to one half of the open wardrobe. She went over to it and jangled some empty wire coathangers. 'Enough?'

'More than enough. Perfect.' Sally looked over to me,

24

as though in apology for an insincerity so unnatural to her.

Stiffly, as though all her limbs were aching, Jutta kicked off her sandals and then carefully stretched herself out on one of the two beds. She gave a little tremulous sigh, almost a sob, and shut her eyes.

Sally went over to her suitcase and unlocked it. As she drew out a silk dressing-gown, given to her by her parents on her last birthday, she asked: 'Did you have this room to yourself? Before I came, I mean.'

Jutta did not open her eyes. Sleepily she murmured. 'No. Everyone here shares. But the girl who was here is now in hospital. Very ill.'

Sally again looked across at me, the dressing-gown over an arm. She raised her eyebrows, as if to say 'What is one to make of her?'

After a while, as Jutta continued to lie out on the bed, her eyes closed, and Sally continued to unpack, I said: 'Perhaps I ought to return.'

Neither of them said anything.

'Goodbye, Sally.'

'Oh, goodbye, Michael. Don't get lost now, will you?'

'Of course I won't get lost!'

'Goodbye, Jutta.'

'Goodbye.' Jutta turned over on the bed, away from us, with a stifled groan.

IV

Three small, furtive, grubby soldiers, one unshaven, were playing cards at a rickety table, its oil-cloth fastened with tintacks, in a corner of the Naafi. Light filtered down murkily on them through a skylight cloudy with dust and grime. Occasionally one or other of them grunted with the effort of deciding what to play, gave a yelping laugh of delight, or shouted out something like 'Got you!' or 'Mine!' as he raised an arm high to fling down a card.

After a lunch of a greasy, grey soup, from which my spoon had dredged up fragments of meat, fat, gristle and occasionally even bone, eight of us members of the English party had slipped away here to swill mugs of over-sweetened tea and to eat chocolate cup-cakes.

'One feels guilty,' Mervyn sighed, as he stretched out his legs and rested his head on the back of his perilously tilted chair, so that his body was all but horizontal.

'Does one? Why?' Harry, the undergraduate from King's, began to lick melted chocolate off his fingers.

'Oh, Harry!' Jessica put out a plump hand to touch him on the knee. 'Think of those poor creatures living, day after day, on the sort of food we had for lunch. *They* can't come in here, can they?'

'Of course they can't. And a good thing too!' This was the first time that I'd seen the girl, large and fierce-looking, with a fringe across her forehead, who'd now spoken. The girl laughed and then bit into a doughnut. When jam trickled out of it on to her chin, she put out a long tongue and retrieved it. 'Squeeze them till the pips squeak,' she said, her mouth full.

I felt an impulse to squeeze her until the jam ran out of her. Then I noticed that Sally had surreptitiously begun to wrap up an assortment of cup cakes, doughnuts and Mars bars in a piece of newspaper retrieved from under her chair. Having completed this task, she slipped the parcel into her rucksack.

'Are you planning a dormitory feast?' Mervyn had also been watching her.

'For Jutta. She looks so thin and exhausted.'

'Don't forget what old Thwaites warned us yesterday. Anyone smuggling things out for the Germans will lose Naafi privileges.'

'I'll risk that.' In her quiet way, Sally has always been one to take risks.

'What's your billet like?' One of the girls, Edna, eyes heavy with mascara and mouth thick with lipstick – 'the chorus-girl' Mervyn had nicknamed her, when we'd first seen her giving peremptory orders to a cowed, elderly porter at Liverpool Street Station – now leaned towards Sally, a cigarette uptilted in her right hand. A cumbersome gold charm-bracelet dangled from its wrist.

'Not too bad. Better than I'd expected. Yours?'

'Oh, I'm still in the hostel. I hope I can stay there. This girl, burbling in ghastly English, came up to ask if I'd like to share her room. But somehow ...' She pulled a face, her voice trailing off. 'Not my sort of person, not my sort of thing.'

'Michael and Mervyn are the really lucky ones,' Sally said. 'I envy them.' But I knew that she felt no real envy.

'You can't call me lucky. There isn't even electric light in that dump above the garage, the windows are thick with cobwebs, and I have to trek across the garden if I want to spend a penny. But Mervyn's O.K.'

Mervyn, his chair still tilted backwards, yawned, stretching his arms above his head. 'Am I? Well, yes, I suppose I am. It's interesting to be part of a family. Even though, as usually with families, one wishes one might have chosen another one for oneself. Certainly, it's better than a student lodging house. But I loathe the lack of privacy. There's Jürgen – he's the one who asked us – and there's also this cousin of his, Heinz – who seems to come in only one variety, sullen. My heart sank when I saw the three beds, so close to each other. It's a large room but so full of furniture, like the rest of the house, that it seems to be small . . .'

'You must have gone through worse in the Army, Mervyn,' Jessica interposed.

'Yes, but that *was* the Army. This isn't. Still, I like Jürgen. Seems a decent sort of chap. Doesn't he, Michael?'

I frowned. I wasn't sure. 'He's all right,' I eventually conceded. At that moment when he'd first approached us, pushing his way through the groups of chattering students, I'd already felt – inexplicably, disconcertingly, annoyingly – a tug of attraction like some treacherous undertow snatching at a swimmer's body as it floats back and forth, up and down, on a sunlit, stagnant expanse of water. That the attraction might be sexual had never occurred to me.

'Was that the tall blond hunk I saw talking to the three of you?' Edna asked.

'Yep.' Mervyn yawned again, arms stretched up above him. 'Like him?'

'Gorgeous!' She turned to the others eagerly. 'Didn't you notice him? He was wearing these shortest of shorts. Why do men in England never wear shorts like that? Why do they have to wear those baggy things, reaching over their knees?' Since Harry was wearing examples of 'those baggy things', she was either being tactless or deliberately malicious. 'He had these blond hairs on his legs. They looked, the legs looked' – she laughed in delighted recollection – 'as though they'd been smeared with honey.'

'Which you'd have just loved to lick off,' Harry said, perhaps to pay her back for her comment on the shorts.

'Oh, please!' She wrinkled her nose. But clearly the idea had delighted her.

Silent as the others went on chattering, I suddenly found myself recalling those legs in every detail.

'What's this Jürgen reading?' Jessica asked. She was always insistent about placing people, like a pernickety librarian determined that every book should rest on its shelf according to its Dewey number.

'Medicine,' Mervyn replied. 'But he's not really interested in it, he told me. He was pushed into medicine because his father's a famous doctor – scientist – and because that way he could put off getting called up. But what he really wants is to be an actor.'

'Well, he certainly has the looks for an actor,' Edna said.

'But that's exactly what's wrong with him,' Sally interposed. 'He's so – so *theatrical*.'

A metal tray under an arm, one of the two tired women from behind the counter had come over to our table. 'Finished with these?' she asked in a clipped, unfriendly voice. Clearly she had little use for our party, out of uniform, reclining sloppily round the table, our upper middle-class voices assertively loud. She began to load the tray with our used mugs and plates.

Suddenly Mervyn jumped up and set about helping her. It was the sort of gesture with which, so often offhand and rude, he would surprise people, particularly those who'd decided they didn't like him. The woman's face, previously taut, relaxed. 'Thanks, duckie,' she said, as he handed her a pile of plates. Then she said: 'You'd be students at this course, wouldn't you?'

29

'That's right,' Mervyn answered.

'For our sins,' Jessica put in.

'Here you are – here's another one.' Mervyn eased a mug on to the by now crowded tray.

'They warned us about your coming,' the woman said. It sounded ominous. She nodded 'Ta' to Mervyn and then, the tray held high under her bosom as though to support it along with the mugs and plates, she strode off between the tables.

From their corner, their game of cards suspended, the puny soldiers had been watching us. One of them now rose and, a pale, delicate hand on a hip, strolled over. He took up his position behind Mervyn's back-tilted chair. He looked at us in turn. 'What are you then?' he eventually asked.

Mervyn cricked his head round and up. 'What are we? Well, that's a poser! I suppose we're human beings.' He appealed to the rest of us. 'Aren't we?'

The fierce girl barked: 'I hope we are!'

'It's really rather a metaphysical question,' Harry said.

The soldier squinted down angrily at the smeared top of the table. He was too limp and weak, like some plant etiolated from long confinement at the back of a potting-shed, to pose any menace. 'Fuck,' he said, in a conversational tone of voice. Then, having turned precisely on his heel, almost as though he were about to salute us, he returned to his companions.

Jessica giggled again. 'Oh, I say!'

'Good question,' Mervyn said, ' "What are you?" It's something I often ask myself.'

When we left the Naafi, it was to find ourselves under a leaden sky, greyish-green in colour, similar to the one which had sagged low over the devastated countryside through which our overcrowded train had travelled by fitful jerks and halts. None of us seemed to know what to do or where to go next.

A bespectacled boy called Keith, often to be seen by himself, now came over. In the Naafi he'd placed himself at a table as far from us as possible, and had then given all his attention to a single cup of coffee and a *Times* crossword several days old. 'What's the p-p-programme?' he asked.

'N-n-nothing till the opening c-c-ceremony at s-s-six in the Aula,' Harry answered, imitating his stutter.

'That'll be a bore.' Edna was ruefully examining a ladder in one of her stockings. 'I might give it a miss.'

'You can't do that,' Harry protested.

'Can't I? Why not? Just you watch me!'

Mervyn took Sally's arm and drew her away. I followed them. 'Let's go and look for Jürgen. Or Jutta.' He waved a vague hand at the others. 'Be seeing you!' The three of us moved off.

When we eventually looked back, the little group were still standing outside the Naafi door, Jessica with a proprietary arm around Harry's shoulders.

Mervyn laughed. 'They'll probably remain there like that – wondering what to do – until this evening's meeting. What a feeble lot!'

'They could be worse,' Sally said.

'They could be better.'

As we crossed the river by the wooden footbridge, gnats whined round our heads. Then I felt a sting on my lip.

'There'll be a thunder storm,' Mervyn predicted.

'Are we going to look for Jutta or for Jürgen?' Sally asked.

I wanted to answer, 'Jürgen'.

Mervyn said: 'Oh, I've had enough of Jürgen for the moment. Besides I want to see your digs.'

'Do you really want to see them?'

'No. But there's nothing else to do. Unless we just lie down here on the grass and have a sleep.'

'Do you remember the way, Michael?' Sally asked. 'I don't.'

'Of course I do.'

But twice, to my chagrin, I led them astray. The first time we fetched up at a municipal rubbish dump, buzzing with flies; the second time at a derelict cottage, no more than a shack, with a huge piebald cat sunning itself, untroubled by our arrival, in the long grass beside its sagging porch. Sally, her face suddenly radiant, hurried towards the cat, stooped and began to stroke it. Slowly it rose, stretched itself, and then pressed against one of her calves. She looked over to us. 'He likes me.'

'Animals always do,' I said.

'Oh, well, I suppose we'd better get a move on.' Sally must have realised that Mervyn, who was totally indifferent to animals, was getting impatient.

'Poor Sally!' Mervyn exclaimed, when at last we arrived at the four buildings set out in their rectangle. 'Looks like a Borstal.'

Sally gave an uneasy laugh. 'I've never visited a Borstal, so I've no way of judging.'

'Neither have I. But it looks as a Borstal ought to look.'

The same girl, in the one-piece, dark-blue bathing-costume, lay out on a blanket on the sunlit grass. Her collar bones and the side of her neck visible to us were shining with sweat. Her toenails, I now noticed, were painted scarlet. She stirred as we walked past her, then abruptly sat up, arms going round her knees. Head on one side, she squinted up at me from under a tousled fringe. Although she had ignored him it was Mervyn who smiled at her. '*Guten Tag.*' I knew at once that he was

32

attracted to her, as I had known it at once on many similar occasions. Like many people who have had no sexual experiences, I was then hypersensitive to the to-and-fro of sexual undercurrents between others.

'*Guten Tag*,' she returned, picking daintily between her left big toe and the one next to it with a forefinger the nail of which was also painted scarlet.

The building appeared to be empty. 'I think the room's this way,' Sally said vaguely.

'Yes, it is,' I confirmed.

As we walked down the long, narrow corridor, our footfalls on the concrete echoed ahead of us, so that it seemed that, as we advanced, three invisible people advanced to meet us. 'Yes, this is it. Number nineteen.' Sally knocked. There was no answer. She knocked again. Then she took a key out of her bag and turned it in the lock. But the door was already unlocked. She gave it a push and went in, to be followed by Mervyn and me.

Jutta lay asleep, hand under chin and knees drawn up, precisely in the same position in which she'd lain when Sally'd been unpacking. 'Jutta!' Sally called. Then more loudly: 'Jutta!'

Jutta jerked up, eyes stretched wide in alarm and mouth open as though a scream were about to burst from it. Briefly, she looked terrified. Then she put the back of her right hand to her cheek, resting it there. She smiled in dazed relief. 'Oh, Sally!' It was only then that she took in Mervyn's and my presence. 'And – you,' she said oddly. Had she forgotten our names? Or was she reluctant to use them?

'Yes, us.' Mervyn gave her the smile, gentle and humorous, which almost invariably won from people the things that he wanted.

Jutta jumped off the bed, pulling down her skirt with

33

one hand while the other smoothed her hair. She gave a nervous gasp of laughter. 'You should not be here.'

'Me?' Sally was amazed.

'No, not you, Sally. Of course you can be here. This is *our* room. Them – Mervyn and Michael,' she added.

'Oh, dear!' I tried to appear disconcerted and contrite.

'It doesn't matter. The Fräulein is out – she goes to practise singing at the church this day.' Jutta pronounced 'church' as though it were 'kirk', conjuring up an image of a group of Scottish elders. 'No one will know. Or if anyone knows, no one will care. Sit, please.' She pointed to the bed.

I perched myself on one of the lockers. Unself-consciously, Mervyn lowered himself on to Jutta's bed and, body leaning forward, clasped his hands together. Jutta stared at him, as though she were not sure whether she liked what she saw. Then she joined him there.

Sally opened her bag. 'I brought you some things.' She drew out the newspaper parcel and began to unfold it.

'Sally!' There was something unnerving about Jutta's squeal of pleasure as Sally revealed cup cakes, doughnuts and Mars bars. It was as though a gift had been brought to some child who turned out to have been starving. Jutta peered: 'But where did you get such things? You did not bring them from England with you?'

Sally laughed. 'Good heavens, no! Only from the Naafi.'

'The Naafi!' Jutta stared into her face, suddenly fearful. 'But is that not forbidden?'

'Yes. But it doesn't matter if it is. Who cares?'

'You must not get into trouble.'

'What kind of trouble?' Mervyn asked. 'The worst thing that could happen would be to be sent home.'

'Perhaps Sally would like that.' There was bitterness, as well as humour, in Jutta's response.

34

'Have one,' Sally urged. 'Go on!' Jutta hesitated. 'Go on!' she repeated.

Jutta carefully selected a cup cake, peeled off its paper, and then bit into it. She screwed up her eyes, swaying from side to side. 'M-m-m-m!' There was a terrible pathos in her abandonment to the pleasure of devouring the dry cake mouthful by mouthful, with a hand under her chin to catch any crumbs. She'd shrunk back against the wall, her legs tucked under her on the bed, as though fearful that one of us might attempt to seize her prize from her. When she'd finished, there were fragments lodged in the corners of her wide, full lips. Her tongue shot out, now to left and now to right, like a lizard's, to secure them. 'Wonderful,' she breathed.

'Try one of the doughnuts,' I urged.

'Doughnuts?' Jutta had clearly never heard the word. Mervyn pointed.

'But you must eat too,' Jutta said, feverishly brilliant eyes fixed on the two doughnuts on the newspaper.

'We ate at the Naafi. These are all for you.' Once again Mervyn gave her that gentle, humorous smile of his.

'For me!' Jutta pressed against her breastbone a hand rough with what appeared to be hard physical labour. Then she looked up. 'But what about Jürgen?'

Mervyn shrugged.

Sally said: 'I'm afraid I didn't think about Jürgen. He's the boys' responsibility. Isn't he?'

'No, no, no, Sally!' Jutta gave a crowing laugh. 'He is *my* responsibility!' Did that mean, I again wondered, that Jürgen was her boy-friend? 'I will keep this for him. And this.' She moved the remaining cup cake and one of the two doughnuts to a corner of the newspaper. 'He has a big appetite. Big man, big appetite!'

Mervyn looked at his watch. 'We'll soon have to set off for the meeting. It's at six, isn't it?'

'Oh, do we have to go? Couldn't we just give it a miss?'

'Oh, certainly we must go, Michael, certainly!' Jutta was clearly shocked by my suggestion. 'Everyone must go. But first you must change, Sally, I think. We must all look our best. Michael already looks fine. But you must put on a suit and tie, Mervyn, I think. Yes?'

'Oh, must I?'

'Yes, I think so, I think so, Mervyn. Yes.'

'Oh, Christ!'

V

The gilt chairs, with their tautly caned seats and spindly legs, were hideously uncomfortable; but at least the eighteenth-century hall, with its high ceiling and floor of grey marble inlaid with lozenges of green, was cool after the heat of our walk.

Jutta, next to me, was in a silk dress with long sleeves, buttoned at the wrists, and a high, frilled collar. She smelled of baby powder – perhaps because, at that period in Germany, any other kind was difficult to obtain. Beyond her, Jürgen was dressed in an ill-fitting, shiny dark blue pinstripe suit, which – so he later told me – had once belonged to his father. It exuded a faint, peppery smell of sweat. Curiously, I found this smell less disagreeable than that of Jutta's baby powder.

Round the hall there hung portraits of eighteenth-century notabilities with heavy, lumpish features under extravagant wigs. As I'd gazed at them, some of them had seemed oddly familiar. Then I'd realised. Of course! These were Electors of Hanover, some of whom had also been Kings of England.

On the dais were ranged some dozen academic figures, most of them elderly, in voluminous robes, black, scarlet and white. When they'd processed into the hall with a slow, weary dignity, the German students had swiftly risen to their feet, to be followed reluctantly by us British. The Rector, leading this Indian file, had been wearing a shoe from which the sole, hanging loose, had slapped regularly on the marble. It had been all too clear that the sound made him feel self-conscious, despite the assumed air of lofty indifference with which, eyes focused somewhere high above the dais, he'd made his way down the aisle.

It was he who spoke first, in a deep, guttural German, for several minutes on end. Then, reading from another script held in a trembling hand, he switched to a halting English, with many mispronunciations ... *Happy to greet guests from afar ... Cooperation ... Renewed understanding ... Wounds to be healed ... Future belongs to the young ... Young belong to the future ...*

Mervyn, eyes still closed, eventually emitted a groan so loud that Sally, next to him, peered across to see what was wrong.

Colonel Thwaites, in a blue serge suit, not his uniform, and a striped shirt with stiff, detachable collar, came next. Pitching his voice like a trained actor of the old school so that its boom reverberated about the hall, he said many of the lofty things that the Rector had said before him, but far more briskly and concisely. He concluded by telling us firstly that it was the British authorities who were, as he put it, 'footing the bill for this experiment', and then that he hoped that there'd be 'some kind of return match in Britain in the future'. At this second announcement, the Germans stirred and smiled at each other, obviously pleased. 'And now,' he announced, gathering up his notes, 'I wish to give the floor to a very distinguished visitor from my country, over here on a tour.'

This proved to be a bishop. Seeing him, young, moustached and dressed in a suit too tight for his athlete's shoulders, as he had processed up the aisle beside Colonel Thwaites, I'd mistakenly assumed him to be another member of the Allied Control Commission.

He, too, like Thwaites, pitched his voice, a plummy baritone, with all the skill of an actor, so that it could be

38

heard, echoing faintly, in every corner of the musty hall. 'I assume that all of you here speak enough English to understand the few words – yes, I assure you, only a few – that I have to say to you this evening. At all events, your Rector' – he looked back over his shoulder at the Rector, who, rousing himself from some private reverie, then smiled back – 'assures me that you do.' He cleared his throat, a fist pressed to his lips as though to stifle a belch. 'After a terrible war that has devastated your country as it has devastated those of the Allies, I think that all of us must be conscious that one priority stands out above all others – that of rebuilding. Rebuilding and not destruction must now be in all our minds and hearts. By rebuilding I don't mean just the rebuilding of houses and hospitals and factories and schools – important, vitally important, though that is. I mean also the rebuilding of lives, in many cases shattered by the hideous circumstances of the war – separations, bereavements, losses of homes and even places of origin. I mean also the rebuilding of our own selves. "None of us is perfect" is something we often say in my country. And if I now refer to the evil that, like a kind of mass madness, overcame the German people under Hitler, that does not mean – I beg you not to think it – that I am unaware of much that has been less than perfect, often far less than perfect, in the conduct of my own people and their allies in the course of this ghastly conflict. The evils exist on both sides, and we of the side opposite to yours can only give thanks that at least we did not fall into the insanity of concentration camps, genocide and the ill-treatment and even torture of prisoners.'

Mervyn shifted in his flimsy chair. He opened his eyes for a moment and then put a hand over them. 'Oh, Christ!' I heard him mutter.

Jutta, leaning forward, lips parted, the lower one

glistening with saliva, was clearly rapt. Jürgen, beyond her, was assiduously picking at some dry skin at the corner of a thumb-nail. Sally had the air of resigned attention of someone listening to an uninteresting sermon in church.

The bishop's voice boomed on: 'I am not one who believes in hereditary guilt. What true Christian could? Nor am I one who believes that the guilty are beyond redemption. What true Christian could believe that either? Where guilt exists, of course it must be expiated, not merely by repentance but by acts that demonstrate that repentance. Terrible things have happened on the soil of Germany, and those terrible things must be acknowledged. Once acknowledged, they can slowly be expiated, and this once beautiful country of yours – the country of Beethoven, Goethe and Schiller – can once again join the community of the civilised nations of the world.'

How much did the German students understand of all this? And with how much did they agree? On the dais the middle-aged and elderly faces, gravely immobile, betrayed nothing. Around me, there were people, like Jutta, clearly absorbed, and there were other people, like Jürgen, no less clearly indifferent, bored or even hostile. Mervyn caught my wandering gaze. He pulled down the corners of his mouth, as though he'd tasted something bitter. Then his lips formed the single word 'Crap'.

The bishop had made a joke, the first of his speech. People were laughing and he too was laughing, the athletic shoulders jerking up and down. But, startled by that 'Crap', I had missed it.

' ... But to be serious. For these – let's face it – are serious times – in their different way, times quite as serious as those that we have lived through, and that so many have died in. As your distinguished Rector rightly said, it is with you, the youth of the world, that the future, for good or ill, now rests. On the understanding and friendship that you can establish between you depends the future of Europe and, yes, even of the whole world. That is why this initiative, the first of its kind to be taken by my country, is so important. Living for two weeks together, talking together, sharing your experiences of the past, your anxieties of the present and your hopes for the future, you will learn, I feel sure, that you have far more in common with each other than ever you realised. You will find the essential humanity within each living soul – a humanity that none of the terrible crimes committed in the recent past can ever have wholly extinguished ... '

I let my head fall backwards, so that I was now staring up at the ceiling, its double line of chandeliers flickering dimly, as I was soon to find that the lights all over Hildingen flickered. With what was almost a conscious effort, I ceased to listen any longer. Instead, I began to wonder about Jutta and Jürgen. Did they feel the guilt, the need for redemption and the desire to expiate of which the bishop had been speaking? Perhaps some day I'd know them well enough to ask them. And had they had any inkling of what had been going on in the concentration camps or the torture chambers of the Gestapo? Perhaps some day I'd know them well enough to ask them that too.

As the bishop, hands clasped before him and head modestly bowed, returned to his seat, there was an outburst of clapping, loud but oddly brief, as though the audience had been roused to enthusiasm and had then thought better of it. A German younger than the Rector, with what appeared to be a tonsure on his round head, now stepped forward and barked out a few words. He bowed, a few people clapped. The ceremony was over.

As we streamed out of the hall, the Germans, far

outnumbering us British, reminded me, in their solicitude about their guests, of a host of people out with their dogs. The dogs strayed hither and thither, to sniff at interesting smells or to romp with each other. Their owners called 'Bill – where are you?', 'This way, Emily!', 'Mike – here, here!' The cobbled square, tilting away from its clock tower, reverberated with such anxious, proprietary cries. The ordinary people of the town, going about their ordinary tasks, stared – as they were to do throughout our visit – at these young foreigners, so different from the foreigners in their uniforms to whom they had long since grown accustomed.

The air was still heavy. Far off there was a dry crackle of thunder, like tinder catching fire.

Mervyn said: 'How could he have spoken like that?'

'The bishop you mean?' Sally said.

'Who else? Awful man.'

Jutta, having heard only 'the bishop', nodded her head vehemently. 'He said much that was interesting for us. It is good that someone should say these things.'

'Too many people have said them already,' Mervyn retorted crossly.

Jürgen laughed. 'Yes, Mervyn is right. Too many. We know such things too well already.' Jutta put an arm through his, but with a jerk he pulled free. 'Do we go to the Mensa to eat?' he asked. 'Not good. But there is nowhere else.'

Thwaites was approaching, bustling along, arms swinging, in a parody of a soldier on parade. It was at Sally that he was gazing, a fatuous smile on his face. 'Well, have you settled in all right?' he asked. Since neither of the others answered, I said: 'Thank you, yes.'

'You are the guest of . . . ?' He looked at Jürgen.

Jürgen nodded. 'Mervyn and Michael are staying in the house of my father.'

42

'And what are you planning to do now?'

It was Sally to whom he had put the question but Mervyn who answered. 'We're going along to the Mensa for something to eat. We had a ghastly lunch there, so no doubt we'll now have a ghastly dinner. Then we'll be glad of an early bed. We still haven't fully recovered from that journey.'

'Oh, forget about the Mensa! Why not come back to my place for a bite? And a drink, of course.'

Mervyn and I looked helplessly at each other. Sally had already turned away. None of us welcomed the prospect of food at the Mensa, but equally none of us wished to go along with Thwaites.

'It's very kind of you, sir.' Mervyn's 'sir' sounded mocking, not respectful. 'But we have these friends with us, our German friends. We don't really think ...'

'No, no! You need not mind about us!' Jutta cried out, at the same moment as Thwaites extended his arms in an all-embracing gesture and exclaimed, 'Well, bring them along too! What could be better? I warned my secretary we might be a dozen or so. Pot-luck, mind you. But the pot will be better filled than at the Mensa, that I can promise you.' He put an arm round Sally's shoulder and then, as though as an afterthought, another round Jutta's. 'Come along! Come!'

When we'd followed him over to his Austin saloon – 'I sent my driver home,' he explained, 'no point in keeping him out' – he opened one of the front doors and asked skittishly: 'Now which of these two lovely ladies is going to sit beside me?'

'Jutta,' Sally said, hurriedly diving into the back.

'Jutta it is then. Can the four of you all manage in the back? It's rather cramped, I'm afraid.'

Sally had by now clambered on to Mervyn's knee, with a lot of the giggling to which she used to succumb at that

43

time. Jürgen put his arm along the back of the seat and stretched out a leg so that his thigh pressed against mine. I squirmed uneasily and then somehow, by placing my back against the side of the car, shifted away.

'We forgot our coupons!' Jutta suddenly cried out.

'Your coupons?' Startled, Thwaites looked sideways at her, as he changed gear. 'What are you talking about? You won't need coupons in my house, dear girl.'

'We have food coupons for the Mensa. For each meal of the Conference. The coupon for tonight cannot be used for tomorrow, each coupon has a date. We should have given our coupons to some others. Then they can eat twice over!'

'Well, it's not too late.' Thwaites halted the car beside a group of students striding along the verge. They appeared to be in high spirits, the Germans singing a folk-song, their arms in many cases linked unself-consciously with those of their self-conscious English guests.

'Give me your coupons! Give me your coupons!' Jutta commanded us. Then she called the students over, waving the coupons in the air through the open window beside her. The students snatched at them with excited cries of thanks.

'Food is what all these poor devils think about all the time,' Thwaites explained as though Jutta and Jürgen were not present. 'Rationing here is far worse than in England.'

'But I imagine that in the Control Commission you're hardly aware of it,' I said.

'Well, let's say we do all right,' Thwaites answered with a laugh. 'As you'll see now, I hope.'

Thwaites inhabited a tall, narrow house, sparsely furnished with what, in its sturdy bareness and blondness, looked like utility furniture brought out from England.

44

The walls had nothing on them except a few photographs, framed in passe-partout, of people whom I assumed to be members of his family.

A pale, beautiful girl, with straw-coloured hair wound about her head like a turban and a high-jutting bosom which looked out of place on someone so thin, met us in the hall, where she appeared to have been waiting for us.

'This is my secretary,' Thwaites said, waving a hand at her. 'Fräulein Knipper. But you must call her Inge, we all call her Inge. Inge, these are three of the English students. Sally ... Michael ... Mervyn.' When he came to introduce Jutta and Jürgen, he slapped his forehead as he exclaimed: 'Well, bless my soul! I'll forget my own name next!'

There was whisky to drink before dinner, in thick tumblers, with water splashed into it from what looked like a hospital bottle. 'This is the stuff for the end of a hard day, isn't it?' Thwaites stretched out his legs and rattled the change in his pocket with his left hand, while his right raised his glass. '*Prosit!*' – as they say here.' He gulped. Then he turned to Jürgen. 'Well, what do you think of our Scotch? O.K.?'

'Fine. Very fine.'

'Have you drunk it before?'

'Oh, yes.'

'What has Trude left us to eat?' Thwaites eventually turned round to enquire of Inge, who was seated on an upright chair behind him and separate from the rest of us. His face was red from the three whiskies that he'd thrown back in quick succession. 'Let's go and have a dekko.' He got up, then stooped and grabbed at Sally's arm. 'Come! I'm sure you're peckish, aren't you?'

'Not all that peckish.'

'*L'appetit vient en mangeant.*'

In the dining-room a round table, covered in a coarse

linen cloth embroidered with crimson roses, was set out with dishes of cold chicken, ham and salami. There was a wooden bowl of undressed lettuce and unchopped and unpeeled tomatoes and, beside it, an outsize jar, of the kind usually sold only to catering establishments, of Heinz's salad-cream.

Thwaites handed Sally a plate, then handed plates to Mervyn and me. He left it to the Germans to get their own. 'Help yourselves. And don't stint,' he added. 'There's plenty more where that came from.'

Jutta speared a slice of chicken on to her plate. She deliberated, wide brow creased in concentration, and then speared a slice of ham. Having again deliberated, she eventually added three slices of salami, and a heap of lettuce.

Jürgen was more delicate, making Thwaites shout out to him, as he poured wine into glasses: 'Take more than that! For God's sake! No need to be on your best behaviour here!'

Inge hovered round us, her beautiful face impassive, with offers of knives, forks and napkins. When she finally came to help herself, she took only salad.

Mervyn and Sally were later to agree with me that the evening had seemed interminable. For most of the time Thwaites held forth. He talked about his life 'in civvy street' as a teacher of French and German at a provincial grammar school – 'one of the oldest and finest in the whole blessed country'; about his work in Hildingen; and, above all, about the Germans. As he expatiated on the last of these topics – 'Of course most of the blighters knew the whole score, whatever they now may tell you' – it was as though he were wholly unaware that there were three Germans among us. Inge and Jutta listened to him in total docility, as though he were talking about a subject that in no way concerned them, Jutta from time to time raising her head from her food and Inge, still seated behind him, staring dreamily out of the window into the night. But Jürgen, with what seemed to be defiance, had picked up a copy of *The Times*, several days old, had spread it out on his knee, over his by now empty plate, and was frowning down at its central pages. Mervyn yawned and yawned again. Sally, with her natural courtesy, tried to look interested.

At last it seemed that we'd stayed long enough to leave without giving offence.

'I'll drive you back,' Thwaites volunteered.

'Oh, no need for that, thank you, sir. We'd like the walk. Wouldn't we?' Mervyn appealed to us.

'But it'll be no trouble, none at all.'

After some argument, the five of us set off on foot down the narrow, empty street, the light from its lamps so dim that at one moment I all but tripped on a cobblestone and would have fallen if Jürgen hadn't grabbed my arm with a sharp 'Take care!'

'I wonder when Inge goes home,' Sally said.

Mervyn smiled. '*If* she goes home.'

'Poor Inge,' Jutta sighed.

'Why poor Inge?' Sally asked.

'Well, it is clear ... ' Jutta broke off.

'What is clear?' Sally pursued.

Jutta shrugged. 'It is nothing.'

Jürgen cut in brutally: 'Inge is one of a large family. Her father was killed at Stalingrad. I have a friend who is a friend of her family, he has told me about her. She must be nice to the Englishman, because then the Englishman is nice to her little brothers and sisters. Simple!'

'Do you mean she's Colonal Thwaites's girl-friend?' Sally asked.

'Oh, Sally, how innocent you are!' I exclaimed. Yet, as

47

a rule, I myself was just as innocent. Perhaps if I'd been a boarder and not a day-boy at my public school, and if our family had not been so close-knit, I'd have been less so.

All at once Jürgen sounded impatient. 'Girl-friend, lover, mistress. Yes. It is an old story. It is called fraternisation. Once forbidden. Now – common.'

At the word 'fraternisation', I felt his hand on my shoulder, through my thin cotton shirt – I had taken off my jacket since the night was so hot – strangely light, strangely thrilling.

'We should not talk like this about Inge,' Jutta protested in a soft, agitated voice.

'Ah, Jutta, Jutta!'

Jürgen's fingers pressed down harder on my shoulder. Then suddenly they gripped it.

VI

We walked the girls to the door of their building.

'Shall we come in?' Jürgen teased.

Jutta pressed a hand to his lips. 'Sh! Too loud! The Fräulein will hear.'

'Does the Fräulein never go to bed?' Jürgen now whispered.

'She sleeps – up there.' Jutta pointed to an open window above our heads. 'She and her dog Pussy. It is strange to call a dog Pussy, no? Pussy is English for a cat.'

Mervyn approached Sally, drew her towards him, and then placed his lips on one of her cheeks, as I had never done in all the time I'd known her. 'It hasn't rained yet,' he said. As he spoke the words, lightning palpitated on the other side of the river, to be followed almost immediately by a prolonged growl of thunder.

Sally gave him a gentle push. 'You'd better go quickly. Before the rain comes.'

Boldly Jutta crossed over to where Jürgen was standing, put out her arms to encircle his neck, and then kissed him full on the lips. With a little laugh she released him. 'Am I a bad girl,' she asked, 'kissing my man for the English visitors to see?'

Mervyn laughed. 'Very bad.' Then he leaned forward and quickly kissed her, also on the lips. 'Bad, bad.'

As we walked home, Jürgen ignored me, talking only to Mervyn. If I said something, it was Mervyn who responded, not he. When we arrived at the house, Jürgen asked me grudgingly if I wanted a lamp or could manage

49

with the candle already in the room. He then asked me no less grudgingly, as though from a sense of duty, if I had all I needed. I assured him that I had.

Alone in the room, the candle flickering behind me, I stood at the window and peered out through the cobwebs at the moonlit house opposite. Lights went on and off – in the hall, on the staircase, in what I took to be the bedroom where Michael, Jürgen and Heinz all slept. The curtains of the bedroom were drawn, I could see nothing of what was going on in it. Suddenly I felt my isolation. They were there, I was here. If I wanted to go to the lavatory at night, I'd been instructed not to attempt to enter the house, which would be locked, but to use the outside lean-to, full of buckets, mops, brooms, crates and packing-cases, beside the kitchen.

I turned away from the window and began to take off my clothes. Then, all at once, I seemed once again to feel Jürgen's fingers on my shoulder, first touching it so lightly, then gripping it so firmly. But I put the recollection away from me, as one might bundle something soiled out of sight into a drawer.

Lying on my back on the damp, sagging bed, the moonlight bright through the uncurtained window, I could not sleep. I threw myself on to one side and then on to the other. I punched at the hard bolster, its cover so heavily starched that it might have been made of cardboard, and then kicked out at the duvet so that it flopped to the floor.

Eventually, with an almost voluptuous sense of surrender, I decided that I should have to do what I usually did on nights of insomnia. I leaned across to the upright chair on which my clothes were resting, and twitched a handkerchief out of a pocket of my trousers.

As I jerked with increasing frenzy, I thought of Sally, of Jessica, of Edna, of Jutta, even of Inge. Then, suddenly, unaccountably, against my will, I thought of Jürgen. I thought of those long, sunburned legs beneath those shortest of shorts. I thought of those strangely cold, strangely pale blue-green eyes, looking down into mine. I thought of those large, strong hands, the nail of the third finger of the right hand black where he must recently have crushed it.

I gave a groan. I drew up my knees. I exhaled a long, single breath.

VII

The two aunts, Marthe and Hilde, sat strangely crowded against each other on one end of the sheer-backed, oak settee, upholstered in a blotched material the colour of red wine long since spilled, that felt scratchily unwelcoming to the touch whenever I myself had sat on it. It was as though someone invisible were at the other end, preventing them from spreading themselves.

Her arms tucked in close to her sides and the wool taut over an extended index finger in the Continental manner, Marthe – who had no English other than a few phrases such as 'Good morning', 'Thank you' and 'Please' – knitted away as though at a task so boring that her one wish was to complete it as soon as possible. Each time that she tilted her head at the completion of a row, her round glasses in their frames of silvery wire would flash with the late afternoon sunlight slanting through the window beside her to lend a sudden ferocity to a countenance otherwise so gentle and soft. It was she who appeared to be in charge of the household, instructing the little old woman, her face wizened under the scarf knotted about her high-domed head, whom I assumed to be the skivvy of all work.

Hilde, who taught English at a girls' school on the other side of the town, had large, knobbly, masculine hands, on the fourth finger of the left of which she wore a thick-banded wedding-ring and on the little finger a signet-ring of onyx set in heavy gold. She was dressed in a dark-blue linen coat-and-skirt, a crisp white shirt, its collar tied like a jabot, and flat-heeled brogue shoes. Two combs held back her looped hair, a tarnished gold, on either side of her wide, determined face.

Behind them sat the Professor, their brother, on the piano-stool, one elbow resting on the piano itself and a chin cupped in a palm. He was half turned away from the rest of us, at once still and distracted, saying not a word. He might have been posing for a picture or a statue – 'Reflection', 'Ennui' or 'World-weary'. Perhaps he was bored with us three English, waiting here for Jürgen, who, as so often, was late.

There'd been a brief, sharp bombardment of hail, melting as soon as it had fallen. Now it seemed as if more hail, or at least rain, were coming. Hilde drew a handkerchief from a sleeve of her jacket and waved it back and forth before her face in an ineffectual attempt at fanning. Why didn't she remove the jacket? All three of the old people seemed to dress without any regard for a temperature that was hovering about the eighties.

Hilde said: 'I do not quite understand. What is it that you do?'

'Do?' It was Mervyn who answered, even though Hilde had been looking at me. 'Do you mean here – in Hildingen?'

'Of course. Where else?'

'Well, we spend part of our time discussing – all of us together. And then we split up into groups according to our interests – medical students with medical students like Michael and Jürgen, students of English literature with students of English literature like Sally and Jutta, classicists with classicists like myself.'

'I see.' Hilde was clearly not impressed. 'And what is it you discuss when all of you are together?'

'God knows! Everything! Nothing!'

Hilde was clearly even less impressed than before. 'Everything, nothing? But that is surely a contradiction?'

53

She was severe, as though with some particularly foolish pupil at her school. Then she smiled with a sudden indulgence: 'Perhaps all this discussion is not the most important part of your visit.'

'Perhaps not,' Mervyn agreed.

'I certainly hope not,' I said.

Hilde looked at me sharply. There followed a silence, in which Marthe's needles, in feverish movement, sounded like the distant clicking of a typewriter.

Mervyn leaned forward, hands clasped between knees. 'You're not from here? Originally, I mean.'

'No, we are not from here. Our family comes from Dresden. My home was in Dresden and my sister Marthe' – she looked sideways at Marthe, who, still knitting away, did not react in any way to the mention of her name – 'lived not far from me. Jürgen has perhaps told you, we are both widows, my sister and I. We could not live in Dresden any longer, so we came here to live with our brother, the Professor.'

'And Heinz is your son?' I'd seen him briefly, a large, tousled youth, a trainee engineer on the railway.

'No, Heinz is not my son.' She sounded almost indignant at my misattribution. 'Heinz is Marthe's son. Marthe also has a daughter, a married daughter, who lives in Hamburg. I have no children – no longer.' She compressed her lips into a thin line. 'Perhaps you do not know what happened to Dresden?' How could anyone not know? 'Dresden was a very beautiful city, one of the most beautiful in Europe, and our house – our house was also very beautiful. Very old too. More than two hundred and fifty years old. Very beautiful, very old.' There was no doubt now. She was blaming us for the destruction both of the city and of her home.

I hesitated between remaining silent and making a defence. It would have been better, Mervyn and Sally

54

both later told me and I myself came to decide, to have remained silent. But, nettled, I couldn't contain myself. 'Coventry suffered in the same way. Perhaps you don't know what happened to Coventry? It had a very beautiful and very old cathedral. It no longer exists. A lot of Coventry no longer exists.'

Hilde stared at me, a hand to one of the tortoiseshell combs that held back her hair. While I'd been speaking, the Professor had swivelled round on the piano-stool, to listen, rigid and intent. His hands gripped each other tightly. Only Marthe, oblivious of what was being said and impervious to the atmosphere, continued frenziedly at her task.

I swallowed, feeling the blood thumping at my temples. 'My parents lost their home in the Blitz. That was in London. They were away and I was away, we were lucky in that. But one of my aunts was badly injured.' It was hateful, this game of unhappy families. I was already wishing I hadn't started on it.

The Professor sighed. A hand rose, as though of its own volition, and sketched a regretful gesture in the air. 'In war, everyone suffers,' he said, as though enunciating some hitherto unacknowledged truth.

'But some suffer more than others,' Hilde said.

The Professor now raised the same hand to place his pince-nez across the bony ridge of his nose. 'Who can measure suffering?'

'Who indeed?' I could see that Sally had now been roused to the same indignation as myself.

At that moment, Jürgen could be heard from the hall. I felt a sudden uprush of joy. 'Sorry, sorry, sorry! I am late! So much to do, so many people to see!' That was, we had by now learned, his usual excuse. He never specified what it was that he'd had to do and whom it was that he'd had to see. He hurried into the room, looked

55

around at us, and then, with an acuteness that in the days ahead was so often to disconcert me, sensed the tension still in the air, like fumes of cordite after a duel. 'What has been happening?'

'Happening? Nothing has been happening.' Hilde twice put a strong emphasis on the word 'happening'. 'We have been exchanging experiences of the war,' she added drily. 'That is all.'

'Better to forget the war,' the Professor muttered, swinging the stool back towards the piano and again putting out an elbow to it, so as to prop up his sideways tilted body.

'That is not always easy,' Hilde said.

'Where is Jutta? Is she not here?'

Mervyn straightened in the chair in which he'd been lolling. 'Should she be here?'

'I told her to meet us here. For our swim. Remember?'

'She told me she was going to lie down for a little,' Sally volunteered. 'Said she had a headache, was feeling tired. She said nothing about joining us. I didn't realise ... '

'Poor Jutta. She is so often unwell or tired,' Jürgen said.

'Are you surprised?' Hilde asked stonily.

Marthe, having completed yet another row, held up her knitting. She laughed out loud, in delight at her handiwork. In German she said something to Jürgen, and he then went over to examine the knitting, rubbing it between the strong, sunburned fingers of one hand.

'Is it for you, Jürgen?' Sally asked.

'Yes, for me. My aunt always knits for me. Never for poor Heinz. It is a sweater, another sweater. But firstly I do not need a sweater at this time of year, secondly I do not want a sweater of that colour of yellow, and thirdly I have far too many sweaters already.'

Not understanding a word that he was saying, Marthe kept nodding and smiling.

'She must love you a lot,' Sally said.

Jürgen shrugged. Then he clapped his hands together. 'Let us go, or we shall be late for our swim, and that will make us late for the opera. We can pass by the dormitory to see if Jutta wishes to come.'

'Couldn't we telephone her?'

'Lazy! Mervyn, you are lazy!'

'Yes, this heat makes me lazy. It makes Michael energetic, but it makes me lazy. Let's walk as little as possible.'

'All right, Mervyn! I will telephone! Even though the Fräulein does not like to have to go to call the girls.'

Jürgen went out into the hall from where we could hear him shouting down the telephone.

The Professor said: 'The telephones in Hildingen are now terrible. Once . . .' He drew a deep sigh.

Hilde leaned stiffly forward to Sally, making the settee creak. 'You share a room with Jutta?'

'Yes, that's right.'

'Jutta is a nice girl. A good girl,' Hilde said firmly, as though in contradiction of something thought but unspoken by Sally.

Sally nodded her agreement.

'What's her story?' Mervyn asked.

'You must ask Jutta that.' Hilde was chilling. 'If Jutta wishes to tell you.'

'Poor Jutta,' the Professor said.

Jürgen returned. His right hand went to the short-sleeved shirt which he was wearing unbuttoned to his waist, to scratch at the curly blond hair revealed at its opening. 'Jutta wishes to come with us,' he announced. 'She still has a headache but she wishes to come with us. Jutta never likes to miss anything,' he added. 'Come, come!' He beckoned to us with both hands, as though he

57

were summoning a trio of recalcitrant children. 'Come!'

I jumped to my feet. I felt suddenly happy and eager. Sally also jumped up, her long, chestnut-coloured plait – how I used to hate that plait, I don't know why – swinging from side to side. Mervyn rose slowly, stretching his arms above his head and then putting a hand over his mouth to stifle an incipient yawn.

'Mervyn is always yawning. I think that maybe, like Jutta, he is tired.'

'All this Teutonic energy!' Mervyn exclaimed.

'Michael does not become tired.'

I felt absurdly pleased by Jürgen's comment.

'Oh, he's so bossy,' Sally muttered to me as we emerged on to the drive. 'And so pleased with himself.' Even then she did not like Jürgen.

At the dormitory, Sally went in to fetch Jutta, while the rest of us stretched out on the yellowing grass hemmed in by the rectangle of buildings. For a long time, eyes closed against the sunlight, we were silent.

Then Mervyn murmured: 'I find Jutta rather odd. Nice – but odd.'

There was a silence. Had the comment angered Jürgen? But then he replied, his eyes still shut: 'She had a difficult time in the war. And after the war.'

'A difficult time?' Mervyn queried.

Jürgen made no response. Motionless, eyes shut, he might have been asleep. Mervyn didn't pursue the matter.

'Well, you've certainly taken your time,' Mervyn greeted Jutta and Sally crossly, when at long last they appeared. He got to his feet, dusting down his trousers. 'How are you, Jutta? Better?'

'Yes, much better, thank you.' Jutta sounded as though she were not sure. There were dark, shiny rings under her eyes. 'Sally gave me some medicine.'

58

'Only some aspirin,' Sally said. Then as now, Sally always travelled with a first-aid box.

Jürgen had taken a crushed packet of cigarettes out of the breast pocket of his shirt. He held it out to Mervyn, who first hesitated and then took one.

'Oh, Mervyn!' Sally cried out. 'You're supposed to have given up. As I am. Remember? We had a pact.'

'Blame Jürgen. A bad influence. He offered me one, I couldn't resist.'

'Oh, Jürgen!'

Jürgen held out the crumpled packet, not to Sally but to me. 'Come, Michael. You would like one too.'

'Would I?'

'You know you would. Come! Be tempted!' He shook the packet gently before me.

I found myself putting out a hand and extracting a cigarette. Jürgen smiled at me. 'See?' There was a vibrant timbre to his voice, which set up an answering vibration within me. 'It is easy to be tempted.'

'How about this swimming?'

Jutta sounded fretful, even angry.

'How well you swim, Michael,' Jürgen said, as the four of us lay out in the late afternoon sunlight on the bank of the river. Strangely, despite the heat, no other swimmers were in sight.

'Almost as well as you.'

'Michael is the only one of us who's any good at sport,' Sally said. 'Mervyn and I are hopeless.'

'But Sally's the more hopeless of the two of us. She can't even hit the easiest ball across a net.'

'I am also not a good swimmer.' Jutta confessed to this as though to some delinquency. 'I did not learn to swim until last summer, when Jürgen taught me.'

'So you and Jürgen have been friends for some time?'
I said.

'Yes, since the first moment that I came here to Hildingen. I was lucky. As soon as I arrived, I met him.'

Jürgen now lay back on his towel, muscular arms
behind his head and eyes closed against the dazzle of the
cloudless sky above him. The hair curling in his armpits,
like the hair on his chest, was golden in the sunlight.
There was an obtrusive bulge in bathing drawers scanty
for that period. Suddenly, I was overcome by a crazy
impulse to put out a hand to touch that bulge. He was
near enough to do so. Then, no less suddenly, I became
aware that Jutta, mouth half open to reveal her small,
uneven teeth, was staring at me in what appeared to be
stricken consternation. Could she somehow have guessed
at that crazy impulse? I looked away, over my shoulder,
at the river.

At that Jutta jumped to her feet and, bending her head
to one side, used both hands to squeeze her short hair.
Her skin was still bluish from the water. Her teeth began
to chatter.

Jürgen opened his eyes and raised his torso on an
elbow. He stared at her. 'You cannot be cold, Jutta,' he
said at last, in a tone that suggested that he disapproved
of the colour of her skin and the chattering of her teeth.

'Yes, I am cold,' she said with a strange forlornness. 'I
am often cold.' She grabbed her towel off the ground and
began to dry herself.

Jürgen leapt up. He went over to her. 'I will help you.
Here!' He snatched the towel from her and began to rub
her vigorously, like an impatient father with a child.

I stared at him. Then once again I averted my gaze, to
look out across the river.

As his hands moved over Jutta's body, it was increasingly obvious that he was getting an erection.

VIII

That evening we had been to a performance of *Fidelio* at the little eighteenth-century opera house behind the university Aula. It had been a surprising and unsettling experience. Who would have supposed that a town of that size – smaller even than Oxford – would have come up with a production so fine? And who would have expected such an audience, in full evening dress, as though for a pre-war gala at Covent Garden?

Jürgen had told us that the male chorus was composed of men who had themselves been prisoners of the Russians. Inevitably, this knowledge had then made it that much more moving when, blinking, they had emerged from their subterranean captivity into the daylight, to sing of their deliverance. As they did so, I had tried – as, recollecting the occasion, I have often tried since – to imagine the conditions in which, in real life, they had lived and nearly perished in the Soviet Union, their precarious journeys back across a devastated Europe to their homeland, and now their attempts to earn a living by singing in the chorus in this exquisitely artificial little building, on a stage that, at that moment, was probably brighter than any other area in the whole town, except an officers' mess, a Naafi or an operating theatre.

As we left, the audience was oddly subdued. Yet, in the crush bar in the interval, the noise had been so loud that it had been necessary to shout to make oneself heard. Jürgen had grasped Sally by the elbow, guiding her through the crowd. I could see, from the way in which she leaned away from him, that she was repelled by his

61

touch. Jutta and Mervyn followed immediately behind him. I trailed last. I could hear Mervyn tell Jutta: 'What an amazing experience! One of the most amazing of my whole life!' Then he added: 'What an amazing people you are! Even the orchestra played its heart out.'

'Yes, our orchestra is good.' Jutta's tone was judicious. Clearly she was as much puzzled as pleased by his enthusiasm.

Jürgen turned to ask us: 'Do you wish to take a bus or to walk?'

'Oh, let's walk. It's such a gorgeous night,' Sally answered.

As always after darkness had fallen in Hildingen, the streets were almost empty. The lights from the alternate lamp-posts – the others had been extinguished – flickered dimly. Leaving Jutta to walk on ahead with Sally and Mervyn, Jürgen had now joined me in the rear.

'Tell me more about yourself,' he said. Already he had gripped my arm. Now he began to stroke the flesh inside it, just below the crook of the elbow, with the tips of forefinger and middle finger.

At first astonished and then panic-stricken, I stiffened at the contact. But I did not pull free. 'Oh, there's so little to tell.' I felt that I couldn't breathe, as in one of those asthma attacks that I was supposed long since to have outgrown. I felt a savage hammering at my temples. 'I've had a very boring life so far. During the war so many people experienced so many exciting things. Whereas I ... My school was evacuated to the West Country – the West of England – where I lived with an aunt. And my father was in a reserved occupation, he's a doctor, so he never went abroad. I think I'm one of those people to whom nothing really happens. I think that the most exciting things that happen to me are in my dreams.'

'And you dream a lot, Michael?'

62

'Oh, yes.' I gave a brief, nervous laugh. 'Constantly. Vividly.'

Hypnotically the fingers continued to stroke my flesh. 'Will you dream of me tonight?'

'Perhaps. Who knows? I might.'

'I hope it will not be a nightmare.'

'No, I don't think a dream of you would be a nightmare.'

Now he put an arm round my waist, drawing me closer to him. The hand that had been stroking the inside of my arm moved to my right cheek. I had an impulse to pull free, then that died. 'I – like you, Michael. Do you like me a little?'

'Of course, I like you.' I was terrified that some passerby would see us, linked so close to each other. I was terrified that one of the others would look round. How could he be so reckless?

'I wonder if you really like me.' He stroked my cheek, then put his lips to it. 'I think you like Sally more. Are you and Sally . . . ?'

What *were* Sally and I? At that time I did not know, I had given it no thought. 'We're friends, close friends. That's all. Like Sally and Mervyn.'

All at once Jürgen pulled me into a shadowy doorway, set back from the cobbled path and smelling of cat piss. He gripped my chin painfully with a strong hand, tilted up my head, and clamped his mouth on mine. Reluctantly, as his tongue pressed harder and harder, I opened my mouth to let the tongue enter. Part of me felt as if a dentist was performing some namelessly horrible operation. Part of me vibrated with pleasure. I could feel his cock hard against me.

'Jürgen! Michael! Where are you?'

Jürgen laughed softly, without answering, his cheek against mine.

'Jürgen! Jürgen!' Now there was incipient panic in the voice, as Jutta called out through the darkness. She, Sally and Mervyn were silhouetted at the top of the hill against a starry sky.

'Yes, yes! We are coming!' Jürgen now called back. 'Michael has had a stone in his shoe.' How glibly he lied! To me, the cock still hard against me, he whispered: 'We had better go. Otherwise we shall upset Jutta, perhaps also Sally and Mervyn.' He began to hurry ahead of me up the hill.

At our approach, Jutta looked searchingly first into Jürgen's face and then into mine, as they were illuminated by the single flickering lamp above us. 'We have been having a very interesting conversation,' she said in a rapid, panicky voice. 'Mervyn has been telling us how Beethoven came to write *Fidelio*. He knows much, much more about Beethoven than I do.'

'That would not be difficult,' Jürgen said. Then he went over to her and took a lock of her short-cut, reddish-brown hair in a hand. 'Come, little Jutta! You are tired.'

'No, no, I am not tired.' But clearly she was. Her voice fell away, as though it had hardly the strength to sustain itself to the end of a sentence, just as she seemed to have hardly the strength to sustain herself to the end of our journey.

Now it was with Jutta that Jürgen walked, his arm around her waist.

'Oh, that was such a wonderful evening!' Mervyn exclaimed, tilting back his head to look up at the stars.

I nodded. Then, after a moment, I said: 'I think that what really excites you, Mervyn, has nothing to do with personal relationships. What really excites you is some aesthetic experience – a visit to Hildingen cathedral, reading the *Oxford Book of Greek Verse*, hearing *Fidelio* performed to perfection.'

'Was it perfection? No, not perfection,' he corrected me with characteristic exactitude, even pedantry. 'Nothing is perfect in this imperfect world, although in some Platonic other world no doubt a perfect performance of *Fidelio* has been laid up for our delight.' He sighed, all at once mournful. 'Yes, yes, you may be right. When I think of the most memorable experiences of my so far ill-spent life, they're almost always of the on-first-looking-into-Chapman's-Homer variety.'

'That's not very flattering for your friends,' Sally commented.

It was a few seconds before he reacted to that. Then brusquely he protested: 'Oh, for God's sake, Sally! You and Michael mean a lot to me. A lot, a lot. You *know* that!'

'I hope we do.'

As we continued to walk on, turning off from the cobbled path to take a dirt one across a meadow that, dry and dusty by day, was now exhaling a grassy sweetness on the night air, the three of us, usually so close, all at once seemed to be immense, wind-swept distances apart from each other.

IX

The next morning I awoke with a sensation not merely of happiness but of joy. It was a beautiful day, we were to go on a picnic, I should yet again see Jürgen.

But as we straggled up a hill, the German men sunburned in their shortest of shorts and the English men so pallid in their baggiest of flannels, I found myself not with Jürgen but far at the rear with Edna. In her wide-brimmed pink straw hat, dipping over an eye, her innumerable bracelets all the way up an arm, and her white-and-black high-heeled shoes, she looked as though she were on her way not to a picnic but to a garden-party. Suddenly she halted, opened the outsize crocodile-leather handbag dangling from her left wrist, and took out a handkerchief bordered with a hem of lace almost as wide as itself. With little dabs she removed the beads of sweat from her upper lip and her forehead.

'Oh, how I *loathe* walking. Don't you? Never do it if I can help it.'

'I rather like it. But not in this heat.'

'Whatever possessed me to come? It was Duffy who persuaded me.'

'Duffy?'

'The Colonel, Colonel Thwaites. That's what everyone calls him. Or so he told me.'

'Really? Why?'

'Search me! Oh, yes, he did tell me some long and boring story about a plum duff at his prep school or his public school, but I honestly couldn't be bothered to take it in.'

'When did he tell you this story?'

'Over breakfast.'

'Over *breakfast*?'

'Haven't you heard? Didn't anyone tell you? I felt sure that Sally would have told you. She's such a gossip.'

'Tell me what?'

'I've moved in with him.'

'Moved in with him?'

'Yesterday I felt I'd had more than I could take of that ghastly hostel. A whole contingent of ATS arrived – the last straw. I had to queue for a bath for hours – and then the bath was filthy. And I had to queue for the little girl's room – and that was filthy too. Clearly some of those ATS have never been housetrained. So I decided that was that. I went to see Duffy and asked if I could go home. Well, you can imagine the effect. No one here does anything alone, and no one here does anything on his or her own initiative. Out of the question, he said. We'd all come together and we'd all have to go back together. But when I persisted, he all at once told me that, if I liked, I could stay with him. So, of course, I jumped at that.' She stopped for breath, a hand pressed to her side. 'Now, believe it or not, I have a large room, with a bathroom all to myself. Perfect! Mind you, I don't think Inge's all that pleased. It's not hard to guess what's going on between her and Duffy, and I suppose she imagines the same kind of thing is going on between me and him. She couldn't be more wrong. He's quite a pet really, but far too ancient and unattractive to appeal to me in the least.'

'Well, you certainly seem to have fallen on your feet.'

'The only trouble is that he does so love to hold forth. Half the time, as when he was telling me about the plum duff, I just don't listen but get on with my own private thoughts.' Again she halted. 'We must have trudged *miles* by now!'

'I doubt if we've even reached the halfway mark.'

'Oh, *no*!' Again she dabbed at her face with the handkerchief. 'Where's your friend anyway?'

'Sally? Or do you mean Mervyn? I think they're up ahead of us with Jutta.'

'Oh, I didn't mean *them*! I meant the gorgeous Kraut.' She gave me a quizzical, coquettish glance from under the cartwheel brim of her hat.

'Jürgen?' I was disconcerted, then appalled. Had she noticed something, guessed something?

'Yes, him. I adore him. In fact, he's the only one of them I'd look at twice. For me he's – well – sheer heaven.' She sighed. 'But I've never managed to get anywhere with him. I can't be his type.' She paused. 'I wonder what *is* his type?' Mercifully, at that moment she broke off, to swing her handbag at a spaniel which, out on sedate exercise with its mistress, had waddled over to us. 'Go away! Go!' she shouted. Then, as the dog slunk off, she turned back to me: 'Horrid looking creature! Even uglier than its owner.'

As we at last breasted the hill, we came on one of the English students, seated on a bench. His grubby left foot, shoe and sock off, lay across his right thigh, while he peered down at it in intense concentration. At our approach, he looked up and gave us a disconsolate 'Hello'.

'What's the matter, Jeremy?' Edna had screwed up her eyes and small mouth in distaste at the sight of the foot.

'I should have taken a stone out of my shoe a long time ago. But I was talking to this German girl – a real smasher – and somehow, what with one thing and another, I never got round to it. And now she's taken herself off with Harry and Jessica – well, really with Harry, but Jessica won't leave them – and here I am with this mighty blister. Look at it!' He stretched out the foot

68

for our inspection. But Edna and I both at once turned our heads away. 'I suppose you don't have a sticking plaster, do you?'

'Not here,' I replied.

'Perhaps I have.' Dubiously Edna clicked open her outsize handbag and fumbled inside it. 'Yes! Hey presto! Well, fancy that!'

Jeremy now used both hands once again to raise the foot, clearly expecting Edna to apply the plaster to it. But she merely dangled it towards him, as though it were something as distasteful to her as the foot itself. Taking it with a grunt, Jeremy bent over, revealing that the back of his long, thin neck was raw with sunburn.

Edna appraised him with a hard stare. Then she asked: 'Why on earth do you wear that tweed jacket in this heat?'

'Because it has my wallet in it.'

'Couldn't you have left the wallet behind?'

'Might have got stolen.' He pressed fingers against the plaster. 'Don't you remember that Colonel Thwaites warned us about leaving valuables lying around?'

'Then you could have put it in one of your trouser pockets.'

'Too big.' He began to draw on a grey woollen sock. 'That feels better. Thanks. Thanks a lot.' Cheerful now, he smiled up at her, as he pushed the foot into a brogue that looked as if it had never been polished since its purchase.

'You know, you could be quite attractive, if you only took some trouble.'

'Thank you,' he replied with docile gratitude.

'I just can't understand people who go out of the way to make the worst of themselves. Why not have your hair cut decently, for example?'

'Is it too long? I meant to have it cut before we came

away but somehow ... You know how it is.'

'No, it's not too long. That's not what's wrong with it. It's just been cut *badly*.' He had now risen from the seat, and the three of us began to move on. 'Take off your coat and carry it,' Edna commanded.

'My wallet might fall out.'

'Well, give it to me then. You trust me not to steal it, don't you? I'll put it in my bag.'

Meekly he handed over the wallet and then removed his jacket, to reveal a soiled aertex shirt.

I realised that Edna had long since grown bored with me – no doubt because she had sensed my lack of sexual interest in her. Even though he was so unprepossessing, Jeremy's company had caused her to walk out briskly, placing her high heels firmly on the tussocks and stones in her way. She no longer complained about the heat and the distance.

'What do you read?'

'Agriculture.'

'I thought you must.'

Clearly he did not regard this as a compliment. 'Why?'

'Oh, you look so typical. The moment I saw you, I said to myself, "I bet he's reading agriculture."'

'And you?'

'Modern languages. French and Spanish. I ought to have gone to France or Spain this vac, instead of wasting time here.'

'Why did you decide to come to Hildingen?' I asked.

'God knows! I get these quite crazy ideas from time to time. And then I regret them.'

'D'you think you'll regret having come on this expedition?' Jeremy enquired.

'My dear boy, I've regretted it already!'

At this point I fell back, until I could no longer hear Jeremy's immature voice or Edna's self-confident one.

They didn't realise that I was no longer with them; or, if they did realise, it didn't matter to them. I halted and looked back at the town far below me in a misty crook of the river. There were some laggards even farther in the rear, a gust of wind from time to time bringing up to me a snatch of their conversation or their noisy laughter. Now I could even see them, as they appeared round the brow of the hill: two sturdy German boys, in short-sleeved, open-necked shirts and sandals, with rucksacks on their backs; a plump German girl, her long, straight blond hair blowing hither and thither; and two English twin sisters, whose names I didn't know, identically dressed in white linen skirts surmounted by dark-blue *broderie anglaise* blouses. When, seeing me above them, they all shouted out to me, I merely waved and hurried on.

At the summit of the hill, there stood a rustic pavilion, with rough-cut wooden benches and tables set out before it. On the other side of the pavilion I could see a dirt road, up which the cars and vans now parked everywhere must have made their way. From the vans the German students were unloading baskets of food and crates of drink, while the English students, making no attempt to help them, sprawled on the benches or lay outstretched on the grass.

Thwaites – or Duffy, as I now thought of him – hurried over as soon as he saw me. On his head he was wearing a jockey-cap which looked at least two sizes too small for it. 'Hello, there!' He grabbed my hand and shook it vigorously. We might have been lone explorers suddenly coming on each other in the heart of an African jungle. 'I decided to come up with the car. Lazy of me, I know. But nothing could persuade me to face that trudge.'

Looking round for Jürgen, I was hardly listening to him.

Perhaps he realised this, since he now went on: 'If you wonder what's become of your chums, they're in the pavilion over there. There are some bogs in it – none too salubrious, which is surprising in this country. Perhaps they're availing themselves of them. I availed myself of the bushes, I must confess. Down there.' He pointed, as though the precise location might be of interest to me. 'You haven't by any chance seen our little Edna, have you?'

'Isn't she here yet? I thought she was ahead of me.'

He rolled his eyes dolefully. 'No sign of her ... I bet you could do with some beer.'

'Yes, I think I could.'

'I'll get you some in a moment. As soon as it's been unloaded.'

'Oh, I can get some for myself. Thank you.'

'All this stuff comes from the Naafi. You're in luck. A German picnic's not much fun, not on the rations on which these poor beggars have to survive.'

The others now emerged from the pavilion. Mervyn was wiping his face on a handkerchief, then he began to wipe his hands. Sally was laughing at something which Jürgen had said to her. To my astonishment, the Professor was behind them.

'I didn't know your father was coming,' I said to Jürgen.

'But of course he must come! After we have eaten, there is to be music.'

'Music?' Sally was aghast.

'Did you not know that?' Jutta said. 'But I am sure that I told you, Sally. There will be a quartet. The Professor will play. It is a pity that Mervyn cannot play too, but it would be difficult to bring a piano up here, yes?'

'After that climb, I don't think I'd have the strength

to play in any case.' Mervyn was edging himself on to the end of a bench already crowded with students. 'I'm out of training.'

'Nonsense, Mervyn!' Jürgen leaned against him, a hand on his shoulder. 'English men often look weak, but in truth they are different, very different. We learned that in the war, to our cost.' He turned and called out in German to the Professor, who had wandered away from us, to tell him to come and sit on the bench.

At the summons, the Professor wandered back. He was wearing a tropical suit of the same faded blue colour as his eyes, a panama hat jauntily tipped over an eyebrow, and white, open-work leather shoes. A malacca walking stick rested over a bony arm.

'Sit, Papa, sit,' Jürgen repeated, this time in English.

Mervyn got to his feet with an audible sigh. 'Yes, sit here. There's just room.' Then, as the Professor hesitated, he added: 'Please! Please!'

The Professor drew a spotted silk handkerchief from the breast-pocket of his suit, shook it out and then dusted the end of the bench with it, like an over-conscientious maid. The effort caused his breath to snort at the back of his long, beaky nose. He slowly lowered himself, as though into a too hot bath, caught my glance, and rewarded me with the kind of radiant smile that, from time to time, changed his whole face. As I returned the smile, my spirit flooded out to him, in all his cultivated, courteous, old-fashioned rectitude.

'Beautiful,' he said, waving a bony hand at the view below us.

'Yes, beautiful,' I agreed.

'I am sorry now that I did not walk with you. I have made this walk many, many times. But the doctor says that now I must be careful.' He pressed a hand, the veins prominent, to his breastbone. 'Heart,' he said. He laughed and then added: 'The old ticker. That is what you say, yes?'

'Heart or no heart, you will live to be a hundred, Papa. All the members of my father's family live for ever,' Jürgen turned to me to explain. 'It is my mother's family who all die young. So what is to happen to me?'

'You seem to take after your father,' Sally said, stooping to scratch at a mosquito bite on her leg. But I knew even then that Jürgen and his father were totally unlike each other.

Jutta, who had seated herself on the grass, her back resting against the bole of a tree, said: 'There is cold chicken, there is cold ham. Bierwurst. Sausage rolls. Salad. A feast!' She'd been closely watching three of the German students in charge of the food provided by the Control Commission, as they unpacked a hamper near at hand.

'Jutta, how much you think of food!' Jürgen playfully reproached her.

'Do we not all? You do! I think that you are being a hypocrite, Jürgen, as so often.'

The old man blew his nose into the handkerchief that he had previously used to dust off the seat. He did so with a trumpeting flourish, as though to draw attention to himself. Then he said to Mervyn, who'd squatted cross-legged on the grass at his feet: 'I enjoyed our playing of the Trout quintet. You play very well. I am surprised that you do not study music.'

'I'd much rather be what people call a gifted amateur than a second-rate professional. I once thought I'd like to become a professional pianist, but then I realised ...'

'Would you not have enjoyed it?'

Mervyn shook his head. 'I don't enjoy doing things unless I can do them better than most other people.'

'Michael! Michael!'

I swung round to see who was calling to me.

It was Thwaites, a tankard of beer in either fist. 'Yours was the first to be drawn from the keg. Mine was the second.' He held out one of the tankards.

'Perhaps Jutta ... Or the Professor ... ' I murmured, embarrassed.

'No, sonny boy. I brought this for you and no one else. Now if our Edna were here ... '

Reluctantly I took the tankard. Thwaites raised his own, threw back his head and drank deeply. 'That's more like it,' he sighed.

Mervyn scrambled up to his feet from the grass. 'I'll go and get some beer for us,' he said crossly. He clearly resented it that Thwaites had handed the second tankard to me.

'I'll come with you,' Jürgen offered.

Jutta had now lain back full length on the grass, her arms crossed behind her head to make a pillow. Her eyes were closed, she seemed to be asleep. Sally was reading a paperback detective-story, as she so often did in company. (Later she was herself to become a writer of detective stories, so helping to pay for the education of our children.) The Professor had begun to talk in German to the youth seated next to him on the bench.

'Let me show you something,' Thwaites said to me.

'What?'

'Oh, I'm not going to tell you what. I want it to be a surprise. Come!' He beckoned with his tankard. 'Come!'

Reluctantly I set down my tankard on one of the tables and followed him down a twisty, stony path, clutching from time to time at a bush or overhanging branch to prevent myself from falling. He stopped. 'It was about here.' There was a dense bush on our left. 'Yes, here. I came here for my pee-pee and then I saw it. Look!' He stooped, one hand to his knee, and peered into the bush.

75

'Look – through there!' I now also stooped and peered where he was pointing with the tankard. There was a nest with three pale-green eggs in it. Somewhere, at the heart of the bush, I could hear a disquietened rustling of wings, and then a shrill squawking over and over again on the same note.

'Know anything about birds?'

'Not really.'

'Nor do I. It would be nice to know what kind of bird that is. I can't see it now but it's making a devil of a fuss. Perhaps we'd better move off. Pretty colour, those eggs, aren't they?'

'Very.'

'Let's sit here for a moment while I mop up the rest of this bitter.' He peered into the tankard and then pointed with it to a cluster of lichen-covered rocks. 'Not very good bitter.' He belched, closing his eyes as he did so. 'Ridiculous that we should bring it all the way from dear old Blighty.' He belched again, this time putting a finger under his nose, as though to stop a sneeze. 'Come!'

In his khaki shorts, reaching below his bony knees, his long white stockings and his white shirt, its sleeves rolled up and its collar unbuttoned, he perched himself on one of the rocks and then repeated: 'Come, come!'

I hesitated, then perched on a rock near to his. I'd been touched by the excitement and awe with which, like a schoolboy, he's shown me the birds's nest. Not really a bad old stick, I decided with all the patronising condescension of the very young.

'It's cooler,' he said. 'These days are so long. It's quite a relief when the sun begins to set.' He sighed. 'Beautiful.' Like the Professor before him, he raised an arm and pointed down at the view, its green already prematurely tinged with the gold of the coming autumn, as it fell away hazily below us. The town was no longer visible, but far in the distance there was a small village, looking as if it were slipping off the hill on which part of it balanced precariously, while the rest of it filled a shallow valley. 'What a perfect countryside! And yet, you know, I find myself longing for my own bit of the Essex–Suffolk borders. Dedham. Ever been there?'

I shook my head. 'Constable country.'

'Full marks.' He might have been speaking to one of his pupils in the days before he became a soldier. 'As you rightly say, Constable country. And Gainsborough country, people tend to forget that. In my book, Gainsborough painted that countryside better than Constable.' He sighed. 'Yes, one gets homesick, you know.'

'How long have you been here?' Suddenly I was no longer seeing him as a figure of fun.

'Too long.' He clasped one of his bony knees between his joined hands and rocked backwards. 'I get sick of this place. It's bloody depressing – if you'll excuse the expletive – when you come to think of it. All right, the war's over, we've knocked them for six, Hitler and his bully boys have had it. One would just like to forget about it now – and forget about *them*. Let them stew in their own juice – or whatever hot water they've got themselves into. One doesn't want to stir up the juice for them – or heat up the water.'

'I find it so hard to believe that all these people ... I mean, take Jutta and Jürgen. Or Jürgen's father, that sweet old professor who was sitting with us just now. I mean how *could* they have ... ?'

'Oh, they could. They did. My brother was one of the first people to go into Belsen. He's never been the same since. A kind of nervous breakdown, you might say. Or spiritual breakdown, that's more like it, it's the spirit that's conked out. He's lost all belief in – no, not God, not human goodness – but in life itself.' Moodily he stared out westwards, to where the sun was beginning to sink in a raw glow. 'I wonder what my wife and kids are doing now. Oh, I expect she's milking, that's what she's doing,' he decided with a glance at his watch. 'She has this small-holding, acquired it as her war-effort. Runs it extremely well. Hard work. I sometimes think she's so happy with it that she wouldn't really mind all that much if I never came back home.' He laughed, as I was about to make the protest which I felt to be expected of me. 'A morbid thought! Perhaps I'm doing the old dear an injustice. But my girls too – they seem to get on perfectly well without me. One, the older, has just started work as a secretary in the local hospital. The other – my favourite – is still at school.'

'No sons?'

'No sons.' He sighed. 'I'd like to have had a son.' Was it, I wondered, as a son that he saw me? Was that why he so often singled me out for attention from the others? He got to his feet and began to dust off the seat of his trousers. 'We'd better go back or there won't be any grub for us. You know how those poor beggars gobble up anything on offer. Oh, I mustn't forget that.' He stooped for his empty tankard.

Whistling tonelessly under his breath, he began to trudge up the hill ahead of me. Then he halted, once more to stare down into the valley. 'Holy smoke! There's our Edna! Way down there, with some chap or other.' He raised his hand to his eyes to shield them from the glare of the setting sun. His body tilted forward, awkward and rigid. 'Holy smoke!' he repeated under his breath. 'What on earth can she have been doing all this time?'

'She told me how much she hates walking. Perhaps she sat down for a rest.'

Still he peered downwards. 'Who's the chap with her? Know him?'

'Someone called Jeremy. You must have come across him.'

'Reading agriculture?' He spoke with contempt.

'That's the one.' In addition to the contempt, I could now sense his dismay. 'He got a stone in his shoe and the stone gave him a blister. So perhaps, like Edna, he also couldn't walk fast.'

'Are they pals?'

'Well, only in the sense that all of us are pals. Being together here like this.'

'Strange bedfellows?'

I laughed. 'Well, hardly bedfellows!'

'You know, it's an odd thing.' He hesitated, as though wondering whether to continue. 'I've got the idea that there's more of the bed thing between young people here than back home. It usen't to be like that, not when I was a student at Heidelberg before the war. Perhaps that's the demoralising effect of defeat.'

'Or the liberating effect.'

'He jerked his head round at me, suddenly alert, as though wondering whether he'd really heard what he thought that he'd heard. Then he was distracted by the emergence of Edna and Jeremy from a screen of bushes below. 'Edna! Silly girl! I told you you'd regret not accepting my offer of a lift.'

Edna slipped off her high-heeled shoes, then stooped to take one in each hand. 'I don't regret it at all. I enjoyed every inch of the walk.'

'Not every inch, Edna,' I corrected her. 'Certainly not the inches you walked with me.'

Edna pouted as she handed her shoes to Jeremy. 'Be an angel and carry those for me.'

Having taken the shoes, Jeremy wrapped them in the jacket which he was already carrying.

'Won't you dirty your jacket?' Thwaites said in a tone

which implied that he'd be only too happy if Jeremy did so.

'Doesn't matter. It's due for a clean. Just as soon as I get home.'

'Where *is* home?' Edna asked.

'Battersea.'

Edna frowned. 'We used to know someone who lived in Battersea,' she said. 'Once.' She was not more specific. She turned to Thwaites: 'Is there something to drink, Duffy? I'm parched. Fortunately we met two Germans – just ordinary Germans, working men, not students – and they had a water-bottle, so I was bold and asked for a swig from it. But of course I couldn't drink too much.'

'There's beer. Lukewarm English beer, just as we drink it at home. I'll get you some.'

'Oh, Jeremy can get it.'

'Where do I go?' Jeremy asked, eager to serve her.

'Up there!' Thwaites pointed. 'Up that path. And while you're about it, you could return this tankard for me.'

Jeremy, his blister still clearly painful, hobbled quickly up the path ahead of us, tankard in a hand and the shoes, rolled up in the tweed jacket, under an arm.

'He's really rather nice,' Edna confided in me, as though Thwaites were not there. 'One could do something with him, if one were prepared to take the trouble. He's perfectly willing to do what one tells him. If it had to be a choice between him and one of those Germans, then I think I'd go for him. Unless, of course, the German were your chum Jürgen.'

Yet again, I wondered if she were being malicious.

Back at the pavilion, we found that Jürgen had managed to commandeer one of the rustic tables. Jutta, Sally and Mervyn were with him. He rose to greet us: 'Ah, there you are! At last! It has been difficult to keep

80

all these seats, you cannot imagine. Come, come!'

'There's also Jeremy,' Edna said. 'He's gone to get me some beer.'

'Fine. But there is no chair for him. He must sit on the grass.'

'Oh, he won't mind that,' Edna said, slipping quickly into the empty chair next to Jürgen.

Two German students, a boy and a girl, with narrow, sharp faces on extremely long necks, were taking round paper plates, napkins and cutlery so twisted and tarnished that it looked as if it had been borrowed from some factory canteen. Gravely they bowed as they handed a set to each of us at the table. Suddenly remembering Jeremy, I ran after them for another set.

'I feel hungry,' Edna announced. 'The first time I've felt hungry since I got here.'

'You must have been feeling hungry last night when you got up and helped yourself to some cold beef from the fridge.' Thwaites was clearly still smarting from her new interest in Jeremy.

Edna blushed crossly. 'Well, if you remember, I got back from that awful seminar without having had anything to eat.'

'Yes, I know, my dear.' Conciliatory, Thwaites put out a hand to pat the one that she had rested on the edge of the table. At the contact she at once withdrew her hand to her lap. It might have been a fly that had settled on it.

Sally turned to me and smiled. 'I seem to see so little of you, Michael. Nice to have you near.'

'But you see me almost every hour of every day.'

'Do I?' She stared at me, friendly and yet wary. Then she gave her clear, happy laugh.

The Professor, who had been sitting silent, hands resting on the crook of his stick and a cheek resting on his hands, began to hum softly to himself. Mervyn took up what he was humming, then sang out the words in his high, white tenor: '*Gesegnet sei, durch den die Welt enstund; Wie trefflich schuf er sie nach allen Seiten!*'

The Professor laughed with delight. 'You know Wolf's *Italienisches Liederbuch*. The Englishman knows it!'

Mervyn nodded. 'When I was still at school I bought all the Elena Gerhardt records. I still have them.'

'What do those lines mean – the ones you've just sung?' I asked.

'Yes, translate, translate!' Sally cried out.

But it was Jürgen, not Mervyn, who translated, standing up and, in a mock histrionic pose, one hand raised to point at the view slowly drifting into a bluish haze, declaiming in an unnaturally deep voice: 'Blessed be he who made the world; How wonderful he made it on all sides!'

Thwaites began to clap and raggedly, with the exception of the Professor, all of us then joined in.

'The song that I like best in the *Italienisches Liederbuch* is the one' – Jutta put her head on one side in an effort to remember it – 'the one that begins "*Mein Liebster singt am Haus im Mondenscheine ...*"' She broke off, doubtful of how precisely to go on.

Jürgen then took up: '*Und ich muss lauschend hier im Bette liegen.*'

'Translate, translate!' Sally again commanded, and this time Thwaites seconded: 'Yes, give us a translation!'

Now it was Mervyn's turn. 'Outside the house my lover sings in the moonlight, And I must lie in my bed and listen.'

'Why doesn't the silly girl get out of bed?' Thwaites demanded.

'Or invite her lover into it?' Sally added, surprising herself more than us by her boldness. She looked down and blushed.

'Because her mother won't let her do either,' Jürgen answered.

'Mothers are not so strict nowadays,' Thwaites said, giving me a look that clearly invited me to remember what he'd said earlier about the morals of the German young.

'And in any case mothers and daughters are often separated,' Jutta said in a small, tremulous voice. She picked up the tankard before her, threw back her head and drained it.

'Jutta, Jutta!' the Professor began to reprove her in English. 'You should not drink so much beer so fast. You know how only a little alcohol makes you' – he hesitated and then concluded on a note of interrogation – 'squiffy?'

'Squiffy!' Jeremy, now seated on the ground at the Professor's feet, turned his head to look up at him and then burst into raucous laughter.

'Is that the wrong word?' the Professor asked anxiously. 'I am sure that when I – '

'No, no! It's absolutely the right word. It's just that . . . Squiffy,' he repeated, and once more burst into laughter.

The Professor turned his head away, both puzzled and pained.

'You're very ill-mannered,' Edna said primly.

Some other German students were now bringing round plates and bowls of food. 'Perhaps we should help them?' Jutta said to Jürgen, clearly not wishing to do so and no less clearly relieved when he told her: 'It is not necessary. There are so many of them already. Leave them to do it.'

'I wish there was a word "private-spirited" that was the opposite of the word "public-spirited",' Mervyn said. 'I'm afraid I'm private-spirited. Thank God for all these public-spirited people.'

With the exception of Thwaites, who said he wanted

nothing – perhaps Inge and his bowed, wrinkled servant were preparing him a late dinner at home – and of the Professor, who speared a token fragment of chicken breast from one platter held out to him and half a tomato from another, we all piled our plates high.

Mervyn peered at Sally's. 'You're doing yourself jolly well.'

'I like that! What about you?'

Jeremy pulled a piece of gristle out from between two widely spaced front teeth and threw it, in an arc, into the bushes. He bit into a roll and, mouth full, said: 'Well, this is a real spread and no mistake.'

The meal over, a girl student, looking prematurely middle-aged because of the manner in which her hair was drawn back tightly into a voluminous bun from a face shinily devoid of any kind of make-up, approached us, calling out: 'Herr Professor, Herr Professor!'

The Professor rose and he and the girl then spoke to each other in an undertone in German.

'What are they saying?' Sally asked, fretful, as so often, at the exclusion that her ignorance of the language imposed on her.

'She says that now they will play,' Jutta replied. 'In a few minutes, after they have taken the knives and forks and plates, they will play for us. I do not know exactly the programme, but I think you will enjoy.'

'I doubt if Sally will enjoy,' Mervyn said. 'She hates music – unless it's Gilbert and Sullivan.'

'Do you mean we're going to have a *concert*?' Edna was incredulous.

Thwaites nodded. 'That's what I heard.'

'Did you hear that, Jeremy? We're going to have a concert. Can you beat it?'

'Well, in that case, let's do a rapid bunk.'

'Can we? D'you think it's possible?'

Although they'd now begun to whisper to each other, I was sitting near enough to hear them.

'Why not? We can pretend we're going to spend a penny and then we can start back for home. It's going to be a ghastly hike anyway.'

Edna considered. Then she nodded and jumped to her feet.

'You've still got my wallet, haven't you?'

'Safe in my bag. Silly!' In a loud voice she announced: 'I must just spend a penny before the concert starts.'

'In the pavilion.' Jürgen pointed.

'Oh, thanks.'

By now the Professor had already gone off with the young girl who'd come to summon him.

'Can you imagine a string quartet playing after this kind of picnic in England?' Mervyn turned to me to ask.

'You are not pleased?' Jutta was anxious.

'On the contrary. I'm delighted.'

Darkness was falling as the Professor reappeared, now carrying his violin. He was followed by the girl, an acetylene lamp in her hands, and then by the three other members of the quartet, a gaunt young man with a shaven head, and two plain, stolid girls, one of them in thick glasses with tortoiseshell frames.

'*Bitte sehr!*' the girl with the lamp said commandingly, setting it down on the ground. She looked at Mervyn and me. 'Please! I must move this table, these chairs.'

Jutta was the first to rise, helping the girl and a boy who had all at once materialised out of the shadows, to carry the table to one side and to set out the chairs for the music-makers. Then she, Sally, Mervyn and Thwaites walked over to a bench, already occupied, and managed to persuade the people on it to crowd together to make room for them. I'd have followed if Jürgen had not gestured to me with his head to come in the opposite direction, where a number of people were already seated or reclining out on a grassy bank.

When we reached it, he told me: 'Wait here. I will get a rug from my father's car.'

The girl who had brought the lamp now returned, staggering under the weight of two music-stands. The boy helper followed with two more. Gravely they set them up. Then they stepped back and surveyed them, heads on one side, as though they were appraising the arrangement of some pieces of sculpture. The boy started to hang the lamp from a branch of a nearby tree. Meanwhile the players had begun to tune their instruments. The Professor said something to one of the two plain, stolid girls, her viola tucked under her plump chin, and then all four of them laughed.

I peered through the ring of lamplight illuminating the quartet, to the benches on the other side. I could just discern Mervyn, his grey linen jacket a pale glimmer next to the even paler glimmer of Jutta's white blouse. Then Jürgen returned. He threw the rug on the ground and, going down on his hands and knees, began carefully to smooth it out, as though it were a table-cloth for a picnic. Satisfied at last, he motioned to me to seat myself. Then he sat down beside me. Even now, as I think of that moment, I experience once again all its mingled excitement, apprehension and joy.

Someone said 'Sh!' and other voices took up 'Sh! Sh!' From the pavilion there came a ripple of laughter, followed by the sound of a woman's voice. At first I thought that the voice was Edna's – it had the same timbre. Then I realised that it was speaking in German. The girl who'd been in charge of the arrangements for the concert jumped to her feet and hurried off. She shouted out something peremptory. A total hush fell. The girl returned to her chair beside the Professor, with a look of self-congratulation. Clearly she regarded herself as being an important part of the quartet, even if she didn't play in it.

As the players, the tuning of their instruments over, struck up, Jürgen leaned close to me, his mouth to my ear and his right shoulder touching my left. '*Death and the Maiden*,' he said, then adding – as though I didn't know! – 'Schubert.' He remained close to me, so that I could feel his breath on the side of my neck, and could smell that peppery odour, by no means unpleasant, of the sweat of his day of tramping in the heat. He pressed even closer.

I fixed my gaze on the Professor, who was playing, despite the music on the stand before him and despite the girl who was turning it over for him, with his eyes shut. If I concentrated all my attention on him, perhaps what was going to happen would not happen – or, if it did happen, I should not be responsible for it. He looked so peaceful, the faintest of smiles on his lips, that he might have been asleep, lost in some dream of his long-vanished youth. Then I noticed how his bony knee was jerking up and down in time to the music, and how, as it did so, the pince-nez on its black ribbon round his neck swung back and forth like a pendulum. At one point, when the girl with the viola played a false note, his eyes opened briefly and a muffled exclamation of surprise or annoyance escaped from him. The girl responded first with an apprehensive glance over her viola and then with a timid smile. But by then his eyes were shut again. For amateurs, they all played remarkably well. I'd not expected that, from the off-hand way in which Mervyn had spoken of them.

All at once, Jürgen was kneeling, not sitting. Turning to face me, he pulled at my hand and hissed 'Come, come!' I wondered if Mervyn, Sally, Jutta and Thwaites, on the other side of the circle of illumination, could see us. I wondered if the people all around us could hear. 'Come! I wish to show you something.' Again he tugged at my hand.

Today I know that, long before that urgent 'Come!' of his, I was in no doubt what it was that would follow. But at the time I somehow managed to persuade myself that, if he were going to show me something, then it was something as innocent as the bird's nest that Thwaites had shown me earlier. I scrambled first to my knees and then to my feet. Jürgen grabbed a corner of the rug with one hand, and my arm with the other. He propelled me, the rug trailing behind us, towards a clump of trees.

At first the pace he set was slow. Then, when we were far enough away from the audience, he broke into a trot, still propelling me before him. In the centre of the clump of trees, he released the edge of the blanket. This time he did not bother carefully to smooth it out. Without a word, he toppled me down on to it, then stretched himself beside me. I turned my head frantically from side to side as he sought out my mouth. When his lips had at last succeeded in fastening on it, I convulsively put an arm round his shoulder. I gave a little whimper. He was on top of me, his cock hard against my stomach. He tore at the top of my trousers, then cursed under his breath in German as he struggled with the buttons.

I squirmed beneath him, I tried to get up.

'*Nein!*' Once again he clamped his mouth on mine.

I could have called out. I could have tried to punch him or knee him. I could have made another effort to get away from under him when he was fumbling with the buttons of his shorts. But I didn't, I didn't. And no future experience of my whole life was ever to be so thrilling. Even now in recollection, so many years after – as I sit out here in the pearly light of dawn, the cat on my knees – the excitement of it thunders through me like a mill-race.

When it was over, he cradled my head in his arms, showing a tenderness that he'd never shown throughout his violent love-making. He pressed my head tighter and tighter to his chest, as though in an effort somehow to fuse our two bodies together. His shirt was open and I could feel the hairs rough and moist against my cheek. 'Well? It was not so terrible, was it?'

It was then for the first time, that I again became aware of the music. The sound was softer than it had been through our love-making. But with an extraordinary hyperaesthesia I could make out every strand of it, hearing every note, however faint, that those amateurs were drawing so carefully, so skilfully and oh, so sadly out of their instruments. I looked over Jürgen's shoulder and could see, far off, the yellow circle of light radiating out from the acetylene lamp suspended from its tree, and the four of them beneath it.

Still on the ground, I began frantically to pull at my clothes. Jürgen handed me a handkerchief and I swabbed myself with that. Then I heard the snap of the buckle of his belt. He was standing over me, legs wide apart. 'Come!' He held out a hand. When he had said that 'Come!' to order me to come here with him, his voice had been peremptory. Now it was gentle.

I struggled to my feet, taking his extended hand. What had he made me do? Christ, what had he made me do? But for years, without knowing it, I had wanted someone to make me do precisely this. He drew me slowly towards him and kissed me. But this kiss was not like his previous ones. He might have been a brother kissing a brother, a father kissing a son. Then, while the music of the quartet grew louder and louder, we began to tiptoe back.

Suddenly he halted and jerked me round to face him. 'All right?' he whispered.

I didn't answer, I only smiled at him. I felt strangely

light-headed, as though with a fever.

He stared at me, his pale blue-green eyes narrowed. 'No one must know. No one.'

I nodded. 'No one. Of course.' But could I, in turn, rely on him not to talk?

At the exact moment when we reached the grass bank where we'd previously been reclining, the music ended. There was a burst of clapping followed by a cry, shrill and clear, of 'Bravo!' from Jessica, who was sitting with Harry on a bench behind Mervyn, Sally, Jutta and Thwaites. The three student players rose and bowed self-consciously. But the Professor, remaining in his seat, merely tapped with his bow on his violin, as though also to applaud them.

'I never realised that that Schubert quartet was so long,' I whispered in Jürgen's ear.

'Don't be silly.' He smiled, his teeth gleaming in the moonlight. 'They finished *Death and the Maiden* a long time ago. That was a movement from a Mendelssohn quartet – I cannot remember which. Didn't you notice the difference?'

'Oh, I was too – too ... ' I broke off, with a vague gesture. All at once I felt an overwhelming desire for solitude, for silence, for complete darkness, for my own bed. 'What comes next?'

What came next was an English boy – from the Royal College of Music, I discovered later – who played to us on the guitar. 'It's what T.S. Eliot called "whisper music", isn't it?' I said to Jürgen. When Jürgen looked blank, I quoted ' "A woman drew her long black hair out tight, And fiddled whisper music on those strings".'

It was the kind of show-off remark that Mervyn or Sally might have enjoyed – and even themselves have made. Stupid to make it to Jürgen, who merely shook his head in incomprehension.

The music over, everyone began to get up. Thwaites hurried across. 'Well, what did you think of that? Not a perfect performance, but a perfect setting. One couldn't have asked for more.'

'No. One couldn't,' I answered. As I said that, I wanted to burst into laughter at the unintentional appropriateness of his comment.

'I think there are buses,' Jutta said. 'For those who do not wish to walk.'

I thought of Edna and Jeremy trudging back together, not knowing of the buses. I felt both sorry for them and amused that they should have been paid out for hurrying off before the concert. 'I certainly don't want to walk. I've had more than enough exercise for one day.' Once again I was thinking longingly of solitude, silence, darkness, my own bed.

It was at that moment that I became aware that Sally was staring at me with a peculiar, squinting intensity, her lips thin. Had she seen something, guessed something? Then, as I returned her gaze, willing myself to betray nothing to her, she gave herself a little shake, as though to arouse herself from a day-dream. 'I think I'll go in the bus too,' she said. 'What about you, Jutta?'

'I could give you all a lift,' Thwaites offered. 'Provided that naughty girl has got herself safely home.' It took me a moment to realise that the 'naughty girl' could only be Edna.

'Oh, I should think that by now Edna must be in bed. But whether with Jeremy, who can say?' Was Sally being deliberately cruel to Thwaites? If so, it was unlike her.

'My father also has his car,' Jürgen said. 'He does not often use it, because it requires so much petrol. But this time he drove here in it. I think I must drive him back. At night he cannot see easily. We must also take with us two of the girls from the quartet. You had better come with me, Mervyn. Sally, Jutta and Michael can go with Colonel Thwaites.' I was surprised and puzzled that he should have selected Mervyn, not me, to travel with him.

'That sounds a first-class arrangement to me,' Thwaites concurred. 'If there's anyone else – I could take another one.' He peered hungrily around at the students.

The Professor limped over, followed by the girls.

'Where is your violin?' Jutta asked him.

The old man answered in German. Then he looked at me and smiled. 'Beautiful music,' he said. 'Schubert.'

I nodded, feeling the blood mount to my cheeks. 'Beautiful.'

'I know nothing of English music,' he confessed.

'There's nothing – or very little – to know,' Mervyn said. 'Don't bother.'

The Professor's car was an old and powerful Mercedes-Benz. Its dark green and black paintwork and its brass fittings glowed under the lamp beneath which it was parked. 'What a terrific car!' Admiringly, Mervyn circled it, inspecting it from every angle.

'In perfect nick,' Thwaites said. 'Who looks after it? You must have a chauffeur.'

The old man shook his head, the pince-nez low on the bridge of his nose. All at once he reminded me of a benign sheep, although I knew even then that there was nothing sheeplike about his character. 'My sister, Hilde, is my chauffeuse. She looks after the car, as though it were her baby. It belonged to our father and now it belongs to both of us.'

I could imagine Hilde passionately buffing the paintwork, polishing the brass, sweeping out the interior and washing the dust and mire off the huge mud-guards and the footplates.

The old man was about to clamber into the driver's seat when Jürgen prevented him, putting a hand, affect-

92

ionate but firm, on his shoulder. There was a brief argument, which ended in the old man pulling a face and then reluctantly getting into the other seat in front.

'Is it all right for you in the back, with the girls?' Jürgen asked Mervyn. 'Take care you do not sit on my father's violin! He would never forgive you.'

A group of students, German and English, had collected admiringly round the car, paying no attention to the increasingly exasperated bleating of the horn of the bus that was to take back those not prepared to walk. 'Gosh! That must guzzle petrol,' Harry remarked to Jessica, hugging her to him. 'I imagine a month's petrol ration goes in a single joy-ride.'

'Goodbye, Colonel Thwaites.' Mervyn went over and shook Thwaites's hand, with that ironic deference of his that bordered on cheek. '*Auf Wiedersehen*, Jutta.' He smiled and waved at her, and in return she uncertainly raised her hand. 'Goodbye, Sally.' To me he said nothing. Was there any significance in that nothing? In my guilt-ridden state, I was prepared to believe that there was. But perhaps, tired and eager not to keep the old man waiting, he had merely forgotten. Or perhaps he assumed that he would see me later at the house.

Jürgen now came over to me. He raised my hand, previously hanging limp by my side, and gave it a gentle press. 'I will see you at the house.' A threat, a promise? Jutta he kissed, first on one cheek and then on the other. He did the same to Sally, before turning to Thwaites. 'We must thank you.'

'Thank me? Good God, what for?'

'For all that delicious food. If it had not been for you ... '

'Oh, not me! H.M.G.'

'H.M.G.?'

'His Majesty's Government. You must thank them.

93

Nowadays it is from them that all blessings flow – or almost all.'

'You will sit in front with the Colonel,' Jutta told Sally, after we'd waved goodbye to the Mercedes and crossed over to Thwaites's far smaller and shabbier vehicle. As so often, she spoke as though giving a command.

'No, no! You get in front. Please!'

Jutta hesitated, then she got in front.

'D'you think that little girl over there would like a lift?' Thwaites enquired.

The 'little girl' was a tall, wide-hipped undergraduate from Girton.

'She seems very happy with those two German men,' I answered. 'But you could ask her if you liked.'

As I'd expected, the girl preferred to stay with her two Germans. 'It's such a gorgeous night for a walk,' she explained.

'A gorgeous night, a gorgeous girl,' Thwaites murmured as the car jerked forward in a series of increasingly violent spasms. 'And I bet they'll have a gorgeous time together.'

I leaned forward from the back seat. 'The handbrake's on. At least, it feels as if it is.'

'Good God! You're right, old boy. Silly old Duffy!' As we now began to gather speed, he set up a whistle, so loud and so shrill that I wanted to put my hands over my ears.

'What is that tune?' Jutta enquired.

'It's an old song, my pet, probably written when you were still only a twinkle in your father's eye. It's called "Yes, we have no bananas", and it's therefore suitable for the present situation in England and even more for the present situation here.'

'Yes, we have no bananas,' Jutta repeated reflectively.

'That's it. Right!' He whistled the tune for a short while

longer and then, as though he'd suddenly wearied of it, broke off in mid-phrase to say: 'Well, that was a jolly occasion, wasn't it? I'm not sure my idea of fun is a string quartet playing some particularly lugubrious music while gnats bite my ankles, but it was fun nonetheless, definitely fun.'

'Jürgen's father's a remarkable old man,' Sally said beside me.

Thwaites peered into the mirror, as though in an effort to see her face. 'Yes, indeed. A remarkable old man.' He added after a pause: 'I think one could say that. He's certainly no fool.'

'He's one's idea of the old, pre-Hitler German. So sane, reasonable, courteous, cultivated,' I said. Then I suddenly realised that this might seem offensive to Jutta, who after all belonged to a later generation. 'Not that there aren't thousands and thousands of sane, reasonable, courteous and cultivated *young* Germans. We've met a lot of them here.'

'I'm not at all sure that there are thousands and thousands of sane, reasonable, courteous and cultivated people in *any* country,' Thwaites said.

Jutta, head turned sideways, was looking out of the window at the moonlit countryside through which we were speeding. Perhaps she hadn't been listening to the conversation. Better that way.

Soon after that our lights picked out a male figure, an arm outstretched, thumb raised, beside the road. Far from slowing down, Thwaites accelerated.

'Was that a hitch-hiker?' Sally asked, peering back through the open window beside her.

'Yes, I think so,' Jutta said.

'Now if it had been a beautiful girl ... ' Thwaites sighed.

There was a silence. Then Jutta said: 'Coming West –

from my old home, after the Russians have come – I took many rides. Sometimes I walked, sometimes I climbed on a train without a ticket or permission, but also I took rides. Often in Army lorries, although it is forbidden. Many, many miles. Many, many days.' She gave a deep sigh. 'Very difficult.'

'I bet it would have been even more difficult if you'd been a boy and not a pretty young girl,' Thwaites commented.

'And were you alone?' I asked.

'Sometimes alone, sometimes with one person or another person. Not friends. Just met. Hello, we say, goodbye, we say.'

As we entered the dimly lit, now misty town – it looked as if it had been shrouded in giant cobwebs – Thwaites volunteered: 'How about a nightcap?'

'Nightcap?' Jutta was puzzled.

'A drink before going to bed,' I explained. Then I said: 'I think we'd better go straight home, Duffy.' It was the first time that I'd called him that, although he'd twice asked me to do so that day. I was sure that Inge wouldn't want us turning up at that hour – or, probably, at any hour. 'I'm tired. And I'm sure the girls are tired.'

'Yes, I am tired,' Jutta said. It was something that she usually denied, even when grey with fatigue. 'I am sorry – tonight no – no *nightcap*.' Once again the jackdaw had appropriated a glittering new word.

'Very well, my dears. Your wish is my command. There are always other evenings and other occasions for nightcaps.'

As Jutta was clambering out of the car, Thwaites grabbed her hand. 'What about a goodnight kiss for the kind man who's brought you all the way to your door?'

Jutta gave a shrill, nervous laugh – more a screech than

a laugh – as she extricated herself from his grip. 'No, no kiss. Thank you, Colonel Thwaites.'

'Cruel, ungrateful girl!' But he didn't seem really to mind. 'Sally?'

Calmly, Sally leaned into the car and placed her lips on his cheek. At once he tried to grab hold of her, but gently yet decisively she pulled herself free.

'Not one on the mouth?'

'I'm afraid not. Sorry.'

'I mightn't have been so kind if I'd known that you girls were going to be so *un*kind. Ah, well, that's the story of my life!' It was without any malice that he waved goodbye to the pair of them.

As we drove off, he said: 'Jolly pair of girls.'

'Yes.'

'I suppose Sally's keen on Mervyn?'

'Mervyn's more keen on her than she is on him. Or so I'd guess.'

'For a time I thought she was *your* girl-friend. Then I realised ...'

What had he realised? But I did not dare to ask him.

'That Jutta's a girl with a story. You can bet your life on that. I wonder what it is. Something tragic, I'd bet.'

By then I was too tired to answer, and we drove on in silence.

Alone, in the small, damp, bare room above the garage, I began to undress. Would Jürgen come to me tonight? I now hoped that he wouldn't. I wanted to obliterate all that had happened, stuffing it into some oubliette, as I had stuffed my soiled underpants into the bottom of my rucksack, under books and a pair of shoes that I still had not worn.

In my pyjamas I stood at the open window. A breeze came through it, the first of that long day. It dried the sweat on my neck and my forehead, it seemed to cool all fevers.

A shadow emerged from the clump of trees at the bottom of the garden and then slowly began to cross the lawn. Jürgen! But no, no, it wasn't Jürgen, as for a moment of terror, excitement and joy I'd imagined. It was only the ancient dog, limping, head and tail lowered, on some secret nocturnal errand.

X

Each day I now craved only to be with Jürgen. When we were separated, I'd find myself constantly thinking of him, so deaf to everything going on around me that more than once Mervyn was driven to shout impatiently: 'Oh, wake up, Michael! For God's sake, wake up!'

During Jürgen's frequent absences – he would never divulge where he was going or where he'd been, but Mervyn complained more than once of being woken up in the early hours when he limped home from (Mervyn's phrase) 'one of his shagging expeditions' – I'd feel, in my lassitude, as though I were convalescing from some long, debilitating illness. But each of his reappearances would at once revitalise me.

There were many times when, bewildered and desperate, I'd ask myself whether our lovemaking on that night of the concert had not all been a dream. Had the gnats really whined around us, had I really sprawled beneath his body, had I really shut out the sounds of the four amateurs playing the Schubert quartet to their rapt audience, had I really struggled for a few futile seconds, succumbed, had an orgasm? Jürgen behaved as though none of all these things had ever happened. It would have been so easy for him to come up to the little room above the garage. He never did so. Indeed, he hardly ever spoke to me, or even looked in my direction.

Frequently I'd try to draw him away from the others; but they – or he himself – would invariably frustrate me. There were Mervyn and Sally; and, worse – since she was so persistent in her constant attendance – there was Jutta.

Once on a walk, when Jürgen stopped to urinate behind some bushes, I managed to hang back – as I thought, unnoticed – in order to be alone with him. But while I stood waiting by the roadside, imagining that the others, nine of them in all, were walking on ahead, I all at once realised that farther up the road, a mere thirty or forty yards, Jutta was waiting too. She never looked in my direction, instead moving her head right, left, up, down, as though, out alone in the country, she'd suddenly found herself to be lost and was searching for a landmark. When Jürgen emerged, unselfconsciously doing up the fly-buttons of his shorts, I hurried close to him and said in a low voice: 'I wanted to be alone with you. I wanted to talk to you. But now ...' With no more than a movement of the eyes, I indicated the small, solitary figure up the road.

Jürgen merely shrugged and smiled. Then he stooped, picked a poppy from the dusty hedge-row, and, with a small, ironical bow, handed it to me before setting off briskly up the path.

I hurried after him. Catching him up, I said: 'Perhaps you should really give this to Jutta.'

He paid no attention. 'Hey!' he called out to her, as she still stood there forlornly waiting. Then he said something to her in German. At once her expression, previously so woebegone, brightened.

'Where are the others?' I asked her, in a tone that implied: Why aren't you with them?

Jutta gestured vaguely ahead. 'They are playing some game. I do not understand it. Some English game.'

'Oh, Mervyn and his idiotic word-games!' But perhaps it was even more idiotic to play people-games, as I was already beginning to suspect that Jürgen did.

*   *   *

Two days later, in the same forest – we had decided to walk to a nineteenth-century folly, a gimcrack replica of the Torre in the Piazza San Marco in Venice – an incident occurred which, to this day, still both puzzles me with its sense of things unacknowledged and even unknown, and infuriates me with its sense of opportunity lost.

Once more I was at the far rear of our party. But this time it was not because I wanted to be alone with Jürgen but because I had decided to take a photograph of Hildingen picturesquely (as I thought) framed by the chestnut trees above a disused quarry. I fussed with the exposure meter and first a yellow filter and then a red one. The camera had been lent to me by my father and, always then in strenuous competition with him, I wanted to show him that I could use it to far more effect than he could.

When I had at last finished, I hurried up the track in pursuit of the others. I remember how loudly the birds seemed to be singing, and how brilliantly the sunlight seemed to be falling, between the branches, in long, diagonal swathes on the reddish soil ahead of me.

Then, all at once, there he was. I was walking beside an impenetrable wall of brambles, wondering if I should halt again to pick some of their berries to relieve my thirst, when what was, in effect, a dark hole appeared in the dusty, green tangle, as though gouged out by a giant knife. Overgrown, here was another, smaller, far more secret path leading off from the one which we were following.

Jürgen stood at the mouth of the hole. He had taken off his shirt. He was wearing those shorts of his, now grubby from long use. His arms were crossed in front of him, the hand of one grasping the wrist of the other, with the shirt, of a military-looking khaki, lying over them. He stared at me. He did not smile, he made no movement. Behind him the tunnel of the overgrown path seemed to

101

pulsate in and out, in and out, as gust after gust of the hot, dry wind blew down it.

I stared back at him. But still I walked on. I walked on so fast that he might have been some stranger whom I suspected of wishing to rob or even murder me. Why didn't I stop? Why didn't I say something? Why didn't he say something? I had dreamed so often of being alone with him. I had wanted it so obsessively.

My pace grew even quicker. Behind me, loudly whistling – some jaunty, commonplace tune, which I could not identify and still cannot, though I hear it even now, all these years later – he followed. I knew that he was following, though I never once looked round.

Why that apprehension of something darkly menacing? Why that perverse self-denial? Why that, yes, panic?

I did not know then. I cannot be sure that I know even now.

XI

One evening there was a dance, attended not merely by
the participants in the conference but by some of the
English officers – the other ranks were excluded – and
some of the Germans working for them. The band was
an amateur university one, its male members all wearing
a uniform of grey flannel trousers, blue blazers, white
shirts and yellow velvet bow ties. Its one female member,
her frizzy, red hair held in place by two tortoise-shell clips
above ears that stuck out slightly, was dressed in a white
ball gown which constricted her ample body as far as the
knees and then flared outwards in wider and wider net
flounces, one frothing above the other. Mervyn laughed
when Jeremy described her as 'glamorous'. Jutta then
looked hurt, clearly taking his derision to be directed at
German womanhood in general. 'I agree with Jeremy,'
she said, frowning stubbornly. 'She is really a glamorous
girl.'

Edna let out a squeal. 'Oh, Jutta, no!'

'What do you think, Jürgen?' Mervyn asked. 'You're
the connoisseur.'

Jürgen replied enigmatically, looking neither at
Mervyn nor at the girl, but at me, across the table from
him. 'She was more attractive last year than this.'

'Do you know her?' Jeremy asked. 'Personally, I mean.'

'Jürgen would hardly have known her impersonally,'
Sally said.

Jürgen shrugged. 'A little. Her mother used to sew for
my mother.'

The girl sang now in German and now in English, her

body jerking in time to the music, while she held her arms rigidly pressed to her sides, the palms turned outwards. The posture looked both unnatural and uncomfortable. The English words, often grotesquely mispronounced, suggested that she'd learned them parrot-fashion from a gramophone record. It was only when she sang in German that her pale face, with its shiny shadows under the eyes, grew animated and sometimes even jolly.

From time to time men from other tables, some whom we knew and others total strangers, would come over to ask Sally to dance. 'Care for this one?' or 'How about it?' the English would negligently say. The Germans were totally different. They would stand before her, feet together, they would stiffly bow, and then they would murmur '*Bitte*' or 'Please', extending a hand. She was the recipient of more of these invitations than Jutta or even, surprisingly, Edna.

I myself did not dance. Instead I surreptitiously watched Jürgen as, indefatigably, he moved about the floor with partner after partner, many of them girls previously unknown to him.

'Why don't you dance?' Sally asked me at one moment.

'Don't feel like it. The floor's so crowded,' I added, as though that were an excuse.

'Won't you dance with *me*?'

I smiled. 'Not tonight.'

'I wish I knew how to dance,' Jeremy said. He had long since removed his jacket, and his shirt had now darkened at the armpits and where, between the shoulder-blades, it was sticking to his back. Clearly piqued that Edna had just returned to the table with her arm round the waist of a lanky German student, his right cheek puckered with a duelling scar, he added roguishly: 'Sally, you must teach me to dance. I think I'd like to have lessons from you. A strict mistress.'

104

Eventually, unable to stand the noise and the heat any longer, I excused myself and went out to the lavatory, which was outside the dance hall. As I was doing up my trouser buttons, I heard footsteps behind me. It was Jürgen. I turned and then, involuntarily, extended both hands in greeting.

He bowed. 'May I have this dance?'

Far off, I could still hear the band playing.

I stared at him.

He laughed. Then he came up to me and took me in his arms.

'Jürgen! Please! Anyone might come in!'

But even as I protested, I yielded to him. As we circled the small space between the urinals and the wash-basins, I was dizzily aware of the closeness of his body, of the responsiveness of his flesh. He pressed his cheek to mine as the far-off singer's voice, raucously amplified in its grotesque imitation of an American accent, throbbed 'Heaven, I'm in heaven ... ' Then he began to hum along with the number, grasping me tighter and tighter. What if someone were to enter? Mervyn, Thwaites, Jeremy, Harry, one of the English officers? Then I ceased to care.

'Oh, Jürgen, Jürgen, I'm so happy now! But I was feeling so unhappy. The time's going so quickly, only five more days, and we seem to see so little of each other.'

He laughed. 'What do you mean? We see each other almost every hour of almost every day.'

'I mean alone, alone. I don't want you shared around with so many other people. You often behave as though they were far more important and far more interesting – '

'Don't talk,' he said with an unexpected gentleness, placing his cheek against my temple. 'Don't. Just hold me. Hold me. Tight.'

I shut my eyes, we strained towards each other. I was

conscious of his hand low on my back, of his other hand in my own, of his breath on my cheek, growing more and more effortful. Then, with a shock of delight, I felt his cock hard against me.

'Oh, Jürgen, when, when can we be alone together, as on the night of that picnic? Why don't you come to my room? That wouldn't be so difficult – '

'Sh! Don't talk. *Nein!*'

When the music had ceased, we separated. 'You go first,' Jürgen said. 'I will come later. Better so.'

Self-consciously I went back to our table and reseated myself.

Jürgen did not appear.

Soon after that the little band struck up 'Auld Lang Syne', to signal that the dance was ending. From table to table, led by the English officers, people crossed arms and joined hands.

'It's not New Year, is it?' Mervyn said, remaining seated.

'Oh, come on, Mervyn!' Edna went up behind his chair and, with surprising strength, succeeded in tipping it so far forward that he fell off it to sprawl on the floor. For a moment he looked so furious that I thought he'd either strike Edna or storm out of the hall. Then he got to his feet and held out one hand to Edna and one to Thwaites.

Surprisingly, Thwaites now extended a hand, the fingers orange with nicotine, to me.

All at once there beside me was Jürgen, to take my other hand in his. When Jutta, with a despairing look on her face, edged round to him, he then held out his other hand to her.

Some of the officers began to bawl out the words, stamping their feet and swaying from side to side. Although there had been only beer on offer, many of them, their faces flushed under close-cropped hair, were drunk. The girls with them screeched, pumped their arms up and down, and threw themselves about with laughter. Group by group, the students now joined in, also stamping their feet and swaying from side to side. I glanced across Thwaites to Mervyn. For once he seemed to be wholeheartedly enjoying the kind of public celebration that usually he loathed. Then I looked across Jürgen to Jutta, whose other hand was grasped by a stocky English officer. Her face had on it an expression of apprehension, almost terror, as she mouthed the song with no audible sound emerging. Sally, between two officers, was tousled and flushed.

Jürgen gripped my hand tighter and tighter as, chest thrust out, he sang in his vibrant, nasal baritone. I couldn't sing. The pain of his grip made me want to cry out and yet, at the same time, it filled me with exhilaration. Later, I'd find a bruise where the ball of his thumb had pressed on the flesh of my own thumb and forefinger.

When the music stopped, people began to embrace each other, men even falling into the arms of other men, since there were many more of them than of women. Jürgen grasped me in his arms, laughing wildly. Then it was Sally whose arms were around me, and her lips that, for the first time since we had known each other, were pressed to my own.

'Happy New Year, darling!' she called out as eventually she let go of me. I realised that she was tipsy.

I laughed. Was she kissing me in joke or earnest? I could not be sure. It was only months later that I knew she'd kissed me in earnest.

'It's all quite mad,' Mervyn pronounced. 'Dotty. All those pre-war songs like "Red Sails in the Sunset" and "The Isle of Capri", and now "Auld Lang Syne" in the middle of August. In years to come we'll never believe it

107

happened. It'll all be like a dream.'

I wanted to cry out: Oh, no, not like a dream, not like a dream!

That night, as on the previous night, the Alsatian dog lay across the foot of my narrow bed. I guessed that she was left out in the garden because, old and frail though she was, she was meant to guard the house. But when, claws clicking on the wood, she'd mounted the stairs behind me, her tail sweeping from side to side, I hadn't had the heart to exclude her. But how could I sleep when she took up so much of the bed and grunted and snored so loudly?

For some reason, I began to think of Jutta. On the one occasion during the dance when the German girl had been on the floor and Sally had been seated, Sally had spoken to me about her.

'It's weird. She's weird. She has this doll, this ancient doll, which she told me belonged to her grandmother and then to her mother, and which she brought with her, all the way across Germany, from the East to here. She calls it "Püppchen". "Püppchen" just means "doll", doesn't it? Sometimes she talks to Püppchen. Püppchen always sleeps beside her, in her arms, like a baby she must protect.'

Sally had gone on to tell me how twice – on her first night of sharing with Jutta, and then again on the night before the dance – she had been woken by Jutta screaming in a nightmare. Sally had jumped out of bed and hurried over. For a long time, sobbing now like a lost, frightened child, Jutta had not seemed to know who Sally was, as she had clung to her, her face pressed against her breast. 'She must have gone through something terrible,' Sally had concluded. 'But what can it have been?'

'Why don't you ask her?'

'How could I? If she wants to tell me, then she can tell me.' Sally, so often impenetrable in her own reserve, has always respected the reserve of others.

Stroking the dog's head, I thought of that look of terror on Jutta's face as, arms moving automatically up and down, she had soundlessly mouthed 'Auld Lang Syne' in the dance hall. But I no longer felt any pity for her, as I do now – knowing from a chance encounter with someone who had been her neighbour, that eventually, many years later in America, she was to kill herself in a particularly horrible manner... At that time I felt only that she was yet another obstacle between myself and Jürgen.

XII

When, over breakfast one day, I happened to let slip that, ever since our gardener had been called up in the second year of the war, it was my mother and I who'd looked after our garden, the Professor at once offered to show me the Botanic Gardens on the outskirts of the city.

I'd have much preferred to go swimming with the others as we'd planned. But how could I say that? Instead, I asked dubiously whether he could really spare the time.

'I have all the time in the world, dear sir. This is the vacation. And, as I have told you, I have now almost retired.' He beamed over his pince-nez at me. 'I am now an old man.'

'Wouldn't any of the others like to come too?' I looked at them in general and at Jürgen in particular, but clearly none of them would. Jürgen said: 'I think it is nicer for you and my father to be alone.'

But, in fact, the Professor and I were not to be alone, since Hilde all at once decided that she would accompany us. 'I need some fresh air. And on the way back I will call in on a friend of mine who keeps chickens and goats. From time to time – she helps us.' At these last words, a flush swept up her neck into her cheeks. No doubt such transactions were forbidden in Germany, as they were ineffectually forbidden back home. 'I will get my hat and umbrella.'

The 'umbrella' was, in fact, an old-fashioned parasol, ivory-handled and covered in a shimmering pale-blue silk fringed with white lace. As she jerked it open as soon as we'd left the shuttered coolness of the house for the heat

110

and dazzle of the open air, it looked grotesquely unsuited, in its femininity and frivolity, to this dour, plain, large-boned woman, with her straight hair, looped up on either side of her wide face, and her flat-heeled brogues.

Perhaps she guessed my reaction to it, since she began to explain: 'My mother's. This umbrella was my mother's.'

I all but corrected her: 'Parasol. Not umbrella.' But by then I'd learned that, however bad their English, the Germans didn't care to have it put right.

Hilde raised a hand in a white cotton glove and pulled down the hat, a straw one such as a peasant woman might wear in the fields, lower over her forehead. 'Should you not wear a hat?' she asked with disapproval.

'I haven't got a hat. Not with me.'

'A hat for the sun is not expensive to buy even now in Germany.'

'The sun doesn't really bother me.'

'You might suffer – how do you say? You might become ill from too much sun.'

'Sunstroke.'

'Sunstroke. Yes.'

'Oh, I love the sun. I can't have too much of it. I feel at my best in it.'

'But sunburn – is it considered attractive in England?'

'Yes I think it is.'

'I myself do not find sunburn attractive. But now in Germany, as you will have noticed, everyone is – is crazy about the sun. Even before the war it was so.'

The Professor was walking ahead of us to the tank-like Mercedes, his gait jaunty in his old-fashioned boots. With his stick he suddenly swiped at a giant plantain growing up between one rose-bush and another. 'So many weeds,' he called over his shoulder. 'Why do Jürgen and Heinz never remove the weeds?'

111

'Because, because! If anyone removes the weeds, I remove them. It is not my job but I remove them.'

'Those boys are so lazy.'

'All boys are lazy. Yes, Michael?'

'Surely not more so than girls.'

There followed a brief argument as to who was to drive the car. 'There is trouble with the clutch,' Hilde said, as though that settled it. 'It is better if I drive.'

'Hilde is such a bully,' the Professor remarked to me, making it sound like a statement of fact, not a joke.

'Someone must play the bully,' Hilde said, with no explanation of why this should be so. She chucked her parasol on to the back seat of the car, next to where I was already seated, hitched up her skirt with both hands, and then clambered in behind the steering wheel. The Professor got into the front beside her, with that familiar wheezing of his as of a kettle coming to the boil.

There were few cars or even trucks on the road, and most of those belonged to the Control Commission. Hilde, who drove fast but skilfully, kept muttering under her breath when some driver frustrated her in her wish to pass, to race a traffic light, or to make an immediate turn. No less frequently the Professor admonished her in German, his profile, with its large, beaked nose, outlined against the yellowing glass of the windshield. Noble, I thought. Not a handsome face, but a noble one.

At the gates to the Botanic Gardens, Hilde blew a double blast on the horn to attract the attention of an old man, in singlet, cloth cap and ragged check trousers held up by braces, who was pushing a hand-mower on a verge. Having recognised the car, he abandoned the mower and at once hurried over. Cap doffed, he greeted us obsequiously, before rushing to open the gates. As Hilde drove through, he raised an arm in what was, in effect, a military salute.

'You're allowed to drive in, then?'

Hilde smiled in satisfaction. 'Some people are, some people are not.'

The Professor explained: 'One of our uncles was a botanist. He came here from Dresden to be a professor – like me. He travelled to every part of the world, and he brought back many plants for this garden. The people here remember that.'

Hilde parked the car under some chestnut trees, their leaves already turning. She didn't bother to lock it. Then she opened her parasol with a decisive flourish. Meanwhile the old man was adjusting his brown Homburg hat to a more rakish angle.

'We shall go first to the orchid house, yes?'

Hilda had other ideas. 'No, first to the temperate house.'

The Professor sighed. 'Very well, Hilde, we shall go first to the temperate house.'

As we made our slow way down a gravel path devoid of any weeds, past flower beds equally devoid of any weeds, and then across a lawn that reminded me of the lawns of Mervyn's Oxford college, Magdalen, I at last exclaimed: 'But it's incredible! After the war! Everything's so beautifully kept. Far better than at any botanic garden I ever saw. How is it possible?'

There was a silence. The Professor frowned briefly, as though at a twinge of pain. Then he said: 'It has not been at all easy. But we love our Botanic Gardens and we were determined that, war or no war, we must care for them as we have always cared for them.'

The Professor's passion was orchids. The sweat beading his forehead and running down the two deep furrows on either side of his beaked nose, he stooped, peered upwards, lifted fleshy leaves, pointed with his stick. Feeling slightly giddy and sick from the heat, I tried

113

to attend to his lecture. 'This is what we call an epiphytic orchid. It is not, you understand, a parasite, since it does not live on the tree but on the air, the water, the – the humus in the crevices of the bark. Very beautiful, yes? ... You notice what we call the pseudo-bulb, yes? ... It is difficult now to obtain osmunda fibre, even to obtain sphagnum moss. These are really essential. But dried bracken, the fibrous bark of fir trees ...' As he droned on, I realised that Hilde had left us.

Suddenly, at the far end of the tropical house, we came on a squat, wild-eyed young man, in ragged khaki shorts and nothing else, who was hosing down some plants. At his first sight of us, he started back, prehensile toes – he was barefoot – gripping at the ridge of symmetrically placed tiles on either side of the walkway. He looked as though his open mouth, twisted to one side by what might have been a premature stroke, was about to emit a scream. '*Guten Morgen*' the Professor said in a voice that sounded oddly reproving. The man grunted. The Professor said something else and then walked on. I followed him.

'What a strange man!'

The Professor did not answer, his head tilted to stare up at the sky.

Hilde was seated on a bench under some trees, resignedly waiting for us. A young girl with a pram was seated on a nearby bench. From time to time the girl rocked the pram with an outstretched hand, crooning in a voice so low that it seemed that even her baby might have difficulty in hearing her.

Hilde peered at me from under the brim of her straw hat. Her legs were inelegantly wide apart, the parasol between them. 'He is tired,' she said. She might have been talking about the baby in the pram, not me.

'No, no, he still wishes to see the ferns.'

114

'He is tired.'

'A young, healthy boy ...'

'He is tired, Friedrich.'

Neither of them thought of asking me whether I was tired or not.

The Professor sighed. 'Very well. Then we shall go home.'

Hilde rose from the bench. 'You have gardens like this in England,' she said, as though, like her brother in the case of the orchids, she was telling me something of which previously I'd been ignorant. 'I remember your Kew Gardens. Very fine. Have you visited your Kew Gardens?'

'Yes, of course.'

'But you do not live in London.'

'Not now. We did before the war. But in any case I think that everyone in England must have visited Kew Gardens at some time or another.'

'My friends in Sydenham had not visited Kew Gardens. Mr and Mrs Archer. All their lives they had lived in Sydenham, and never had they visited Kew Gardens, until I made them go with me.'

I could imagine Hilde coercing this couple, previously happy never to have set foot in Kew, into making a journey of which they loathed every moment.

'Now I will drive,' the Professor announced as we approached the car.

The sun had moved so that its slanting rays had baked the leather of the driver's seat. I wondered if this was the reason for Hilde's ready acquiescence. 'Yes, you may drive if you wish,' she said with dignified condescension. 'Maybe I shall sit in the back with Michael, so that he does not feel lonely.'

Having got into the car, the Professor shifted uneasily on the seat. 'Ach, it is so hot in here!' he exclaimed peevishly. 'Put down your window, please, Hilde.'

115

'I am already doing so.'

I too was struggling to lower my window with a handle unaccountably stiff.

As the car crawled off, Hilde removed her hat, to reveal damp strands of hair sticking to her forehead above the deep red indentation left by the brim. She waved the hat back and forth before her face. Her legs were again wide apart, the parasol between them, so that I had to huddle into my corner to avoid contact with her. She said something peremptory in German to her brother, and he replied irritably in English: 'I have not forgotten, I have not forgotten.' I assumed – in the event, rightly – that she'd been reminding him about the visit to the friend who kept goats and chickens.

We turned off the highway, to bump up a dusty, uneven track, with meadows, burned brown by the exceptional heat and drought of that summer, undulating away on either side. Although it was now past four o'clock, the glare was so dazzling that, looking out of the window beside me, I wished not for the first time that I'd brought dark glasses with me from England.

Eventually we turned into a driveway, which rose, dipped and rose again before arriving at what was more a shack than a house. Logs of wood were piled untidily to one side of it, and from the other side an invisible dog, presumably tethered to a kennel, could be heard rattling its chain and barking. Hilde half-rose from her seat, leaned forward across her brother, and pressed her finger on the horn, holding it there for several seconds on end. The noise of the dog became even more frenzied. If this was, indeed, the friend of whom they'd spoken, then she must be one with whom they were used to being peremptory.

Eventually the door opened and a pallid, lethargic girl, a baby on her hip, came out, blinking at the glare. Slowly, one might almost have thought reluctantly, she came over to the car. Hilde put her head out of the open window, and the two women began a conversation. If the words seemed to rap out from Hilde as from a typewriter, in the case of the girl they seemed to be dreamily inscribed in the heavy air with a blunt pencil. The Professor, having taken a scientific journal out of the car pocket beside him, was absorbed in reading it, the pince-nez again low on his nose and his breath wheezing in his chest. All too plainly he wanted to disassociate himself from the whole transaction.

The girl gave a final nod and wandered off. The child on her hip had been so still that it might have been a wax model in imminent danger of melting in the heat. Hilde said something clearly disapproving to the Professor. With no response, he went on reading. She repeated it, with more emphasis, and he replied with a weary: '*Ja, ja, ja.*'

Hilde turned to me. 'It is better to deal with her husband. But he is out in the fields, bringing in the goats.' She waved a hand in the direction of the meadows through which we had passed. 'Or so she tells me.'

Without the child now, the girl emerged from the house with two brown-paper bags, one held in a hand and the other, the bulkier, bundled under an arm. Hilde clicked open her purse. Then she said something in German to the Professor, who fumbled to extract his worn crocodile-skin wallet from his inner breast pocket. He drew out two notes and, with a resigned sigh, passed them back to her. Hilde added two notes from her purse and then passed the whole wad out through the window.

There was a clumsy moment as the girl tried to take the money without allowing either of the two bags to fall. Hilde eventually solved the problem by opening the door beside her, half getting out, and taking the bulkier bag from under the arm of the girl. With the hand now freed, the girl took the money and then handed across the other bag. She slipped the notes into a pocket of her faded apron, saying so softly that it was almost a whisper: '*Danke, danke.*' Hilde said nothing as she placed one of the bags on the seat between herself and me and the other on the floor.

The girl watched us drive off, an arm up over her forehead. Clearly she'd raised the arm to shield herself from the sun. But as she stood there, her bare knees together and her blond hair hanging in wisps to her shoulder, I could almost persuade myself that she'd raised it to shield herself from an imminent blow.

'Merely to keep alive now one must waste so much time,' Hilde said. 'My sister does not care, she would prefer to starve than take too much trouble. And Jürgen and Heinz, although they eat, eat, eat, they do not care. Near the office of Heinz there is a butcher. I say to him, Be friendly, go to his shop, talk to him. They were classmates, you understand. But Heinz says, Oh, he is too boring. If one is hungry, does one care if someone is boring or not?' Although Hilde now gave me a piercing look of interrogation, I could think of no answer to the question. 'Yes,' Hilde resumed, 'life now in Germany is very difficult. You may use your Naafi, the Commission provides extra food for you. But for us ... No, you cannot understand.'

I wanted to tell her that life was also difficult in England and that it had been even more difficult in the countries either occupied or devastated by the Germans. But it was too hot, I was too tired, and – yes, I have to admit it – I felt unaccountably in awe of this brisk, solid, determined woman, with her mannish hands and shoes and her deep, imperious voice.

The Professor must have decided to return by a route

different from that taken by Hilde. We were now driving alongside the river, glittering briefly and then darkening and growing hazy as it flowed beneath overarching trees. On an impulse I said: 'I think I'll get out here if I may. I may find the others. We always come to swim somewhere near here.'

The professor slowed the car and then brought it to a standstill, with a squeaking and grinding that suggested that internally all was not well with it, however, immaculate its exterior.

'But you have no bathing costume with you,' Hilde said sharply.

'I expect I can borrow one.'

'But it will be wet, if it has been used.'

'Perhaps I can borrow one that hasn't been used. And if it has, well, in this kind of heat that won't really matter.'

'As you wish.' Hilde's mouth was set in a line. She was clearly put out by my abrupt desertion.

'Maybe we can all get out to look for them,' the Professor suggested. 'There is shade here, it is cool.'

To that Hilde replied crossly in German. Clearly she didn't approve of the idea – perhaps merely because it was her brother, and not she, who'd come up with it.

I watched them drive off. Hilde was still in the back of the car, ramrod stiff, so that the Professor at the wheel might easily have been mistaken for the elderly chauffeur of some local *grande dame*. Although I'd effusively thanked them for showing me the Gardens, I knew that I'd certainly offended Hilde and might even have offended the Professor. I was sorry for that.

When I'd wandered a short distance down the river, I realised that this stretch of it, although superficially similar to the one I'd visited with the others in the past, was in fact different. For the most part the water here was shallow over reefs of jagged stones. Where it was not shallow, it was pocked with slime-dark, stagnant pools, in which weeds wavered hither and thither like strands of long grey hair. I took off my gym-shoes and for a while, perched on a rock, immersed my feet in the water; but it was so warm that it brought no relief. I jumped down from the rock and, shoes in hand, began to walk along the bank, intermittently stumbling on some tussock or hidden stone or root. Eventually, my feet growing sore, I put on my shoes again. Gnats were whining fretfully about me, and from time to time I'd feel a sharp sting on bare legs, arms or the back of my neck. It was these gnats that eventually made me decide to leave the river bank and return to the road.

I'd been wearily trudging along it for several minutes – I'd hoped to take a bus or hitch a lift, but nothing had come along in either direction except an old man high on an even older bicycle and an Army truck crammed with brown-faced English soldiers – when, all at once, as I turned hopefully at the chug of a car-engine behind me, there was the hoot of a horn, followed by a shout of 'Michael! Michael!' The car screeched to a stop, and Thwaites was looking out, his scant hair blown hither and thither by a sudden, dry gust of wind. 'Dear chap! What on earth are you doing here?'

'If you give me a lift, then I'll tell you.'

'Of course I'll give you a lift. Couldn't believe my luck when I saw you trudging down the road ahead of me. Thought I must be dreaming. I was getting so bored with my own company. Hop in, hop in!' He leaned forward and opened the door. In comparison with the soldiers, he looked pallid and fragile, like a patient who's spent many days in bed in a curtained room.

I told him of my visit to the Botanic Gardens with the Professor and Hilde. 'Everything was so tidy,' I concluded. 'In perfect order. Unbelievable.'

'That's because there was no shortage of labour during the war.'

'No shortage?'

'Slave labour. You can imagine how hard those poor beggars worked. It was a case of either sweltering in the Botanical Gardens or being fried to a cinder in a concentration camp.'

'But that doesn't explain why today – three years after the war – everything's still so perfect.'

'Oh, they found a good alternative. Men – and women too – from the local asylum. You could call that slave labour too, I suppose. But actually it's the best kind of therapy for many – perhaps most – of them. Better certainly than these ghastly lobotomies that have become even more popular here than back home.'

'That explains it.'

'Explains what?'

I told him of the muscular, farouche, near-naked man recoiling from us, like some trapped beast, in the tropical house. My memory of him remains vivid even today.

Thwaites nodded. 'Yep. Probably one of them. Not dangerous,' he added. 'They wouldn't allow anyone dangerous out. But I'm surprised he was there on his own, with no one to supervise him.'

We were nearing the town, the sun now an incandescent ball wrapped in trailing scarves of orange and yellow haze. 'How about a drink?'

I was dubious. 'At your place?'

'Well, actually, I was thinking of a little beer garden not far from here. I mean literally a garden. The beer is good – light and chilled.'

I considered for a moment. I longed to be with Jürgen. But who knew where he was at this moment? It was possible that he hadn't gone to bathe with the others in the river, and it was no less possible that he wouldn't

121

turn up that evening. 'All right,' I said at last. Then, thinking that that might have sounded ungracious, I added: 'Yes, that's fine. Thank you.'

At the beer garden Thwaites gave our order in rapid German to a middle-aged man, presumably the owner, who had managed to be both obsequious and surly in his initial reception of us. We were seated at a round cast-iron table painted a bilious yellow. Our chairs were also of cast-iron but unpainted and blotched with rust. Thwaites had gallantly spread a handkerchief on mine before allowing me to sit on it.

'Do you often come here?'

'It belongs to a cousin of Inge's. That man who came to take our orders. Yes, I come here with her, and sometimes also on my own.'

The man returned with the two mugs of beer on a tin tray. He muttered '*Bitte*' as he set them down, so carelessly that beer from mine splashed over the rim. Thwaites said something sharply to him in German – victor to vanquished. 'Well, how's it going?' he then asked me.

'It all depends on what you mean by "it".'

If 'it' was this terrible, unassuaged longing for Jürgen, then 'it' was hardly going well.

'The whole visit,' Thwaites said, gulping at his beer.

'Oh, fine. It'll be something to remember.'

'Well, that's better than something to forget. Something to forget – that's what I feel about my own stay here.'

A woman had emerged from the door of the square red-brick house to which the beer-garden was attached. She stood staring at us, a hand raised to her eyes. 'Oh, Christ!' Thwaites exclaimed. All at once I realised that it was Inge.

'Isn't that Inge?' I said.

At the same moment Inge began to walk towards us.

She gazed at Thwaites, ignoring me. Then she came out with a rushed sentence in German, with all the breathlessness of someone who has raced up a flight of stairs to deliver an urgent message.

'But you've no business to be here,' Thwaites replied coolly in English. He looked at his watch. 'Not yet five. Who's in the office?'

Inge shrugged. Then she said: 'Walther?' giving the name an inflection of hesitant questioning.

'You must know if he's there or isn't. I particularly told you to hang on until my return. There may be a call from Hanover, and you know that Walther – *if* he's there, which seems to be doubtful – will only bungle it. Your sister may or may not be ill, that's not the point. You have a job – which you're damn lucky to have, and which most of the population, male or female, of this stinking little town would be only too happy to take over from you – and you should do it properly or not at all.'

Inge stared at him in mingled humiliation and rage, blinking her slightly protuberant eyes as though sand had been blown into them, until all at once a tear formed along the lower lid of the left one. She gripped her large, worn handbag – perhaps she herself had worked its *gros point* of pink and white cabbage roses against a dark-blue ground – tight in both her hands, as high-pitched, angry German words all at once cascaded from her. On all the previous occasions that I'd met her, she'd been almost wholly mute.

Thwaites raised a hand. 'Please,' he said in English. 'Please, Inge. Please!' That final 'Please!' at last stemmed the torrent. 'Even if that's the case, I fail to see why you should be *here*, when your sister lives on the other side of the town. How do you explain that?'

The whole of Inge's face face seemed all at once to converge on the mouth, which bunched itself together, nose all but touching chin. Then it opened and a single monosyllable exploded from it in German. '*Schwein!*' She raised the bag, hesitated for a moment, as a would-be suicide might hesitate for a moment before launching herself off the topmost ledge of a sky-scraper, and then, leaning over the table, swung it against Thwaites's cheek.

Thwaites remained calm; having lowered the hands that he'd lifted to ward off any further assault, he now spoke with an icy severity in German. Inge backed away. Then, with a snorting sound from the back of her throat, she turned and rushed back into the house.

Thwaites raised his beer mug in a wholly steady hand, sipped meditatively from it, and looked across at me. He smiled. 'Silly girl. To put her job in danger like that. She won't find another half as good. She might not even find one at all. I think it must be because the red rags are showing. That always makes her ratty.'

'The red rags?' I'd never heard the phrase.

'Her time of the month. The curse. Women often get ratty – or batty – then. We have one of these scenes regularly – as regularly as she has the curse, which is not all that regularly.' He gave a brief laugh.

'You haven't sacked her, have you?'

'Oh, good God no! She's far too useful. I'm used to her. And I'm – I'm fond of her. All in all, she's a *bon oeuf* our Inge.' Again he sipped at his beer. 'Yes, from time to time we have one of these firework displays. Of her making, of course. But they pass, they pass. I think that she *needs* them, odd though that may seem to you.'

I looked across at him for a moment. Then I turned my head and stared at the small, square, red-brick house into which Inge had rushed. I imagined her seated in there, in what was gloom after the brightness of the garden, clutching her outsize handbag and sobbing over those *gros point* cabbage roses. Her cousin, the owner of the establishment, would admonish her. She should be careful, she didn't want to lose her English officer, did she? After all, he wasn't a bad sort, and think what he'd done in one way and another for her and the family. At that she would take a handkerchief out of the bag and first blow her nose into it and then, screwing it up into a ball, dab at those slightly protuberant pale-blue eyes of hers. Poor Inge! I wanted to go in to her. But if I did, what would I say?

'Another?'

I shook my head.

'Sure?'

'Sure. Thank you. I'm not much of a drinker.'

Thwaites rose and, hands in baggy flannel trousers, ambled over to the door of the house. He opened it and shouted out in German. Inge's cousin appeared, bowing his close-cropped head in ironic submission as he wiped his hands on the apron that reached almost to his ankles. Thwaites drew a note from his wallet and handed it over. When the German pulled up one side of his apron to give him the change from his trouser pocket, Thwaites waved impatiently at him to indicate that he should keep it. The man again bowed his head in ironic submission, murmuring '*Danke, mein Herr.*'

'*Andiamo!*' Thwaites cried out jovially as he walked back to the table.

'What about Inge?'

'Inge?'

'Mightn't she like a lift?'

'Oh, let the silly cow find her own way. Much better to leave her time to cool off by herself when she gets into one of these paddies.'

'Poor Inge.'

'Oh, there's nothing "poor" about Inge – not even in the material sense, if one compares her lot with that of the majority of Germans at the moment. She's well able to look after herself, is our Inge. Oh, yes, indeed!'

As we drove down the highway, the air cool on my forehead and bare arms through the window beside me, Thwaites began to croon: 'Heaven, I'm in heaven,' suddenly bringing back to me, with a painful jolt, as of something sharp and heavy shifting within me, that moment in the lavatory of the dance hall when Jürgen had placed his cheek against mine and had sung along with the distant girl vocalist. Clearly Thwaites was in a good mood. Perhaps scenes such as the one that I'd just witnessed put him in a good mood – why not? There are many people who enjoy scrapping as much as I loathe it.

He broke off. 'It was so weird to hear that girl singing that number. Somehow one doesn't associate Fred Astaire and Ginger Rogers with this bally country.'

'Yes, weird.' I was now dreamily recalling the nearness of Jürgen's body to mine and that hard cock pressing, pressing, pressing against me.

Suddenly Thwaites said: 'I'll show you something. Got a moment?'

'Well, I ought to ... ' The memory of the dance had given an even greater urgency to my desire to be with Jürgen.

'Won't take a moment. Interesting. Something interesting for you.'

He swung the car off the highway, down a cul-de-sac at the end of which there was a long, low Nissen hut oddly painted with alternate stripes of green and white. He parked so close to its entrance – I was sure that no German would have dared to park like that – that anyone who wished to go in or out would have difficulty in edging past. He pushed at the door and then, holding it open, said with a smile: '*Après vous, Alphonse!*' I went in.

126

It took me some time to become accustomed to the gloom of the hut, its only light slanting through windows in urgent need of a clean. Then I became aware of the notice-boards not merely along the walls on either side but in parallel lines down the centre. Before these notice-boards people were crowded, for the most part in silence, often on tiptoe, heads uptilted, in order to read them better. They might have been examining manuscripts on display in a museum.

'What is it? What are they looking at?'

Thwaites grasped my arm. 'Missing persons. I sometimes think that half of the people in this benighted country are missing. Everyone is looking for someone else. Names are posted here, thousands and thousands of them, in alphabetical order, and day after day people crowd in, searching, searching, searching.'

All at once he looked oppressed, even haggard, at the thought of all those people in constant quest of each other after the cataclysmic upheaval that had scattered them in all directions, as an earthquake scatters pebbles.

A bent, elderly women, her head bound round and round with a scarf, called out excitedly to an old man examining the board next to hers: 'Gottfried, Gottfried!' The old man hurried over to join her, all but slipping on a crack in the linoleum covering the floor, and peered where she was pointing with a hand crooked with arthritis. He raised a forefinger and ran it under the lines. His lips moved silently in his absorbed face as he read. Then, disappointed, shoulders sagging, he turned away, muttering something to her. She, too, shrugged, a hand to the scarf-turban on her head.

Thwaites, still holding my arm, just above the elbow, shepherded me the length of the hut – from time to time he banged into people or caused me to do so – to a door, which he then opened without knocking. A plump, white-haired woman, in a grey coat-and-skirt with a single rope of pearls, looked up from her desk. 'Colonel Thwaites,' she said with a faint French accent. She did not sound welcoming.

'This is Madame Crécy.' Still grasping my arm, he propelled me forward. 'Madame Crécy, this is Michael – Michael Gregg.' He turned to me. 'Have I got the surname right?' I nodded. 'A young Englishman – attending our conference at the university. I told you about our conference. In fact, I'd half hoped you'd come to our opening ceremony.'

The woman rose, carefully screwed the top on to the slim gold fountain-pen with which she'd been writing, and placed it neatly in a tray on the desk. Then she took my hand in hers, giving me a rueful, understanding smile which seemed to be saying: He's all right, but he can be a nuisance, can't he?

'Madame Crécy is Swiss. She's with the Red Cross.'

'You have explained our work here?'

For some unfathomable reason Thwaites answered her in German: '*Natürlich.*'

Madame Crécy turned to me. 'So many people come here, many, many. Not easy.' She shook her head, with its stiffly waved grey hair, and put a plump, carefully manicured hand to the crisp cotton of the collar of her blouse. Then she sighed: 'Sad.'

There seemed to be nothing more for any of us to say. But Thwaites remained there, his head tilted to one side as he blatantly peered down at a file open on the desk. Madame Crécy picked up her fountain pen and unscrewed its top again. Then she drew the file towards her, away from his gaze, with a small smile.

'Sorry. A habit.'

Madame Crécy gave the same small smile, as at the peccadillo of the child of a friend. 'A bad habit.' The playfulness of her tone did not wholly conceal an under-lying disapproval.

Thwaites sighed. 'Yes, I know, *chère madame*. I have so many bad habits.'

A tentative knock at the door – it might have been merely someone accidentally colliding with it in passing – came as an obvious relief to Madame Crécy. '*Kommen Sie!*' she trilled.

The door opened and around it appeared the head, wrapped in its scarf, of the old woman who had for a few moments been so excited by what she had discovered on one of the notice-boards and had then been so disappointed. With repeated bows, she edged into the room, followed by the old man, presumably her husband, dressed in a shiny black suit, with a frayed black tie pinched into a tight knot at the stiff collar of a shirt which, I suddenly realised to my amazement, was made of thick flannel. The old woman spoke with nervous rapidity in German. As she did so, the old man kept nodding his head.

Madame Crécy turned to Thwaites. 'You must excuse me. I must deal with this lady. She has an urgent problem.'

'Yes, yes, of course.' But it was clear that he was reluctant to take his leave. Pointedly Madame Crécy went to the door and held it open. Only then did he move.

Outside he turned to me. 'Are you as inquisitive as I am? Oh, I'd love to know why those two wanted to talk to her.'

'Presumably because they couldn't be sure about that notice.'

'Yes, of course, of course. But are they looking for a missing son? A brother? Nephew? Friend?' He sighed. 'Ah, well, I suppose we'll never know.' He walked ahead of me down the central gangway between the high notice-

129

boards. As I followed, I glanced from time to time at the mostly ragged, famished-looking people crowded before them. I felt the unreasoning guilt – after all, as Thwaites had once remarked to me, the Germans had 'bought it' – that was so often to afflict me during that visit.

Switching on the ignition, he turned to me to say: 'Of course most of them will never come back. But they don't believe that, those poor sods in there. The Crécy woman knows that, and her helpers know that, and *we* know it. But those poor sods don't. They'll be coming here for years, as they've already been coming here for years, in a constant state of hope.'

'Well, I suppose a constant state of hope is better than a constant state of despair.'

He looked gloomy, as he sat hunched over the steering-wheel. 'I'm not so sure about that.' He stared into space. Then he asked: 'Where now, sir?'

I looked at my watch and, as I did so, he leaned over to look at it too. Before I could answer his question, he exclaimed: 'Gosh! Omega!'

'Yes, my father gave it to me as a celebration present when I got a place at Balliol.'

'Your old dad must be rich.'

'Not really.'

'Then he must be very fond of you.'

Was he fond of me? I'd never been sure. I'm not sure even now.

'I think I'd better go straight to the university. We've a meeting at half-past six. It's not far off that now.'

'Your wish is my command.'

'But there's no need to take you out of your way. Just drop me off somewhere convenient for you.'

'I said – your wish is my command.' He leaned forward and pulled up his trouser-leg, head on one side to peer out of the windscreen as he drove with one hand. 'Some-

130

thing's bitten me,' he pronounced, beginning to scratch at the silvery white flesh of a shin. 'I shouldn't be surprised if I've picked up a flea from one of those people in there.'

'Oh, surely not! I thought the Germans were so clean.'

'It's not so easy to be clean if the only way to have a hot bath is to go to the public wash-house, and if soap is so scarce as to be a luxury.' He stopped scratching, to examine his middle finger-nail, which was now smeared with blood. 'I've made myself bleed.' Mournfully, he wiped the finger on the side of his jacket. 'So what are you going to discuss this evening?'

'Oh, the ever-interesting topic, I suppose. German guilt.'

'I can see it no longer interests you, however much it interests the others.'

I shrugged. 'The odd thing is that it seems to interest the German side even more than it interests ours.'

'Side? Interesting you should use the word, when the war's over and everyone's now talking about reconciliation. D'you feel it's a question of opposing sides? Is that how you still see it?'

'I think that's how most of the Germans still see it.'

XIII

I was early for the meeting. There was only one person in the hall, a tall, handsome girl, with an engaging look of being prepared to welcome any fun that came her way.

'Michael!' She jumped up from the desk at which she had been slumped, head resting on it.

I couldn't remember her name. 'Hello.'

'D'you think anyone else is coming?'

'We're early.'

'I'm always early. I wish I could break myself of that habit. Really I suppose it's because I'm afraid I may miss something.'

'I'd willingly miss this.'

At that moment a group of students, German and English, burst in. One of the German boys was brandishing an envelope above his head, which one of the English girls was attempting to snatch from him. 'Oh, give it back, give it back! It's private! Don't open it! Don't read it!' The girl was like a terrier bouncing up and down to retrieve a ball held high out of reach.

'Oh, give it to her, Werner,' one of the other German boys said in English.

'Yes, give it to her, Werner, before she has hysterics,' a laughing English girl seconded.

'Very well. If you say "Please Werner, may I have my letter?" then I will give it to you. Yes?'

Once again the girl jumped up in the air in a futile attempt to retrieve the letter. 'I'll do nothing of the kind!' she cried out. Then she put out a hand and grabbed her tormentor by the genitals. He let out a squeal and several of the girls did likewise. 'Kathleen!' the girl who had been talking to me cried out, more delighted than shocked. Werner had dropped the letter.

Now more and more students were flooding in, the majority of them toting bathing costumes wrapped in damp towels. The skins of many of the English, once waxen and pallid, had now become a raw scarlet from their hours in the sun. People began to flop down at the desks. An English girl, having taken a comb out of her bag and pulled it through her damp hair, then handed it to the German boy with her.

Edna scampered in alone, saw me, waved and hurried over. 'Duffy told me he'd had a lovely afternoon with you.'

'I'd have hardly called it lovely. Rather depressing, in fact.'

'Well, I suppose it was lovely for the poor old thing. I think he's lonely. Inge can't be much fun.' She looked around her. 'Where are the others?'

'I imagined you were with them.'

'No. I decided I must get my hair done. Inge recommended this man opposite the Post Office. Like it?'

'Yes, I was thinking how terrific it looked.'

'It cost absolutely *nothing*. A real screamer – one wonders how he survived the Nazis – but he certainly knows how to cut and set.' Was she again trying to get at me? I couldn't be sure.

Jutta, Jürgen, Sally and Mervyn were almost the last to turn up. Jürgen and Mervyn were so engrossed in talking to each other – they appeared to be having some kind of argument – that they totally ignored Edna and me. Jutta sat down at the desk next to mine and took a nail-file out of her bag. Sally, seeming deliberately to avoid me – or was I again being hypersensitive? – walked to the other end of the hall, a paperback detective-story, as so often, in her hand. Once there, she began to read.

The lean, pale German youth, a history student, who was to chair the meeting, crossed awkwardly over to the dais, mounted it, slipped behind the desk, and then cleared his throat loudly as a signal for quiet. 'I think that you know the programme for this evening. Eric Friend will first speak to us about his ideas, and then we shall discuss. Yes?' He looked round at us, one or two people nodded, and Jessica called out 'Super!' Jutta went on filing her nails, Sally went on reading, and Mervyn and Jürgen, seated directly behind me, went on talking to each other, in voices so low that, however much I strained, I could hear only a word or a phrase – Goethe, elective affinities, romanticism – here and there.

Eric Friend, Wykehamist son of an ambassador, had the reputation of being the most brilliant of all of us. He'd won his scholarship to New College when barely seventeen, and it was said that he'd already been offered a fellowship, which he was dubious about accepting. He hurried over to the dais at a trot – he always seemed to be in a hurry, whatever he was doing – leaped up on to it, and then perched on the edge of the desk. In his over-precise, reedy voice, he began: 'Ladies and gentlemen – or should I say girls and boys?' There were a few half-hearted titters. 'Or friends?' Now everyone was silent, as he looked around him. 'I thought that today I might set the ball rolling by saying one or two things about German history. I don't mean immediate German history, because we've been talking continually about that ever since we first got together.' With an impatient flick of the wrist he brushed away a lock of hair that had slipped across his high, shiny forehead. 'What I had in mind was a retro-spect. Yes, that's what I want to – er – share with you, my ideas about Germany's democratic past.' Sally was still reading, Mervyn and Jürgen were still whispering to each other. Jutta replaced the nail-file in her bag, and then clicked the bag shut, causing Jessica to frown disapprovingly at the noise. 'My main thesis will be this. In countries like, well, Italy or Greece, when there has been an interruption of democracy, when there has been a period of dictatorship, a totalitarian rule' – again the wrist flicked at the obtrusive lock of hair – 'it is the period of dictatorship, the totalitarian rule, that has been the anomaly. Despite Mussolini and despite Metaxas, Italy and Greece are essentially democratic countries.' He paused, chin lowered and eyes gazing at the floor, as though in consideration of his own proposition. Then he went on, with renewed conviction: 'Yes, essentially, Italy and Greece are democratic countries. But of Germany the same cannot be said. In Germany, it is democracy that has always been the anomaly, the aberration. Let us look – let us look for a moment – at the history of the Weimar Republic. The Weimar Republic may in two senses be called an anomaly, an aberration. Yes, in two senses ... '

My attention began to wander. Jutta, her head resting on arms crossed on the desk before her and her eyes shut, looked as though, always so easily exhausted, she had fallen asleep. Behind me, Jürgen and Mervyn had at last stopped muttering. Sally, her book tilted to the light from the window beside her, read on. Edna was scratching with a long, pointed finger-nail at the surface of her desk, as though she were attempting to score her name there. Jeremy was doodling, head on one side, on the cover of the notebook that he always brought with him to meetings, even if he rarely wrote in it or, indeed, opened it. How the Germans were reacting to this lesson in their own history, delivered with so much glib assurance, by an arrogant young man from a country that had so recently been an enemy, there was no way of telling since

135

their faces were as impenetrable as the curtained windows of the Hildingen houses when we walked home after nightfall. Was their common reaction one of hostility? I thought so, but could not be certain. After all, it was possible that I was merely ascribing to them emotions that I myself would have been feeling in their situation.

When, at long last, Eric Friend had finished, his usually pale face flushed and his shirt sweat-soaked as though from an exertion far more strenuous than delivering a paper, he gave a little bow to the chairman seated behind him and then another to the audience, even though at these meetings there was never any applause for a speaker. The chairman rose awkwardly, twisting his head from side to side – he might have been attempting to ease some muscular pain in his neck – and all but knocking over his chair, which he rescued with a lunge. 'Do you have any questions? Yes?'

There was a silence. All the Germans, as if by agreement, were staring down at their desks.

'Yes?'

Jeremy shuffled to his feet, cleared his throat and opened the exercise book on the cover of which he had previously been doodling, as though to look in it for what he wanted to say. But all I could see were more doodles of pin-men, heavily bewhiskered cats, and triangles and circles, one within the other. 'Something occurred to me.' Again he peered at the exercise book, before he went on: 'This whole conception of democracy. May it not be – how shall I put this? – that the trouble is that there is no agreement between countries or even between individuals as to what precisely democracy *is*?' Again he stopped, this time to look not at the exercise book but at the people around him. The Germans looked back at him gravely. Many of us English – having long since decided that dear old Jeremy was really rather an ass – smirked at each other or, in a few cases, even at him. 'Do you see what I'm getting at?' Suddenly he sounded insecure and nervous.

'Perfectly,' Mervyn replied from behind me. 'Crystal clear. You have a remarkable gift for making the most difficult things intelligible.'

There were titters, in which even some of the Germans now joined.

Tremulously, Jeremy continued: 'You see, what we English mean by democracy – with our centuries-old tradition of parliamentary government – may be something totally different from what the Russians mean by it or what – well – the French mean by it, or the Americans, or – or, indeed, you Germans.'

'Sit down,' Mervyn muttered.

But Jeremy struggled on, as though in the belief that not to do so would be cowardice.

When at last he'd finished, the chairman turned to Eric Friend: 'Any comment?'

Eric, again perched on the corner of the desk, spidery fingers laced and head cocked on one side, had been listening with an expression of ironic patience on his long face. Now he gathered himself, rose and turned towards the chairman. 'No. I'm afraid I've no comment to make on that.'

The chairman nodded. 'No comment.'

'Poor darling,' Edna whispered to me, as Jeremy, head lowered and exercise book now tucked under an arm, trailed back to his seat.

'Anyone else?' the chairman invited.

Harry, always voluble, hurried up to the dais, Jessica watching him with intent admiration. He spoke, as he invariably did, at so low a pitch and at so fast a rate that only half of what he said was audible even to me in the front row. He wished, he announced, 'to take the economic view' – that, at least, everyone heard – and it

137

was the economic view that he then proceeded to take for minutes on end, now reading from a prepared statement and now improvising with frequent hesitations and repetitions.

When he'd finished, Eric declared that he had no comment to make on that either.

The meeting then fizzled out, with the chairman again and again asking with increasing insistence whether there was anyone who wished to make a contribution, and the students paying him and Eric Friend less and less attention as they began to chat among themselves.

'Perhaps this heat has shrivelled your brains,' the chairman concluded playfully in his excellent English.

'Or perhaps they've become waterlogged from all that swimming in the river,' Eric added.

A few people tittered. 'Indeed, yes,' the chairman said. Again he looked round at the faces that were now, almost without exception, turned away from him. 'Well, it seems as if I must call this meeting to a close. Thank you, Eric, for a discourse which I think that we would all agree was – er – thought-provoking.' He turned to nod at Eric, who put in: 'Even if it has failed to provoke anyone to thought.' The chairman went on: 'We are very grateful to you, very grateful indeed.' Now he rose, crossed over to Eric and, heels together and body leaning forward, shook his limp, reluctant hand in his strong, eager one.

'I need a drink,' Mervyn said, as we emerged from the lecture hall.

'I also need a drink.' Jürgen threw a comradely arm around Mervyn's shoulders. 'I will buy you a drink, Mervyn.'

'No, no! *I* will buy *you* a drink, my dear chap. After that "discourse"' – he put the word into mocking inverted commas – 'that's the least an Englishman can do for a German.'

Then, without saying anything to Jutta, Sally or me – Jeremy had already claimed Edna – the two of them strode off.

'Are we allowed to join them, do you think?'

Jutta took my question seriously. 'Oh, yes, Michael, surely! I think that they expect us to come too. No?'

We followed them down the corridor, often having to make detours round knots of excitedly chatting students, and entered the Mensa, with its oppressive smells of cigarette smoke, cabbage and carbolic disinfectant. Jürgen had seated himself at a table, while Mervyn, holding a book of the coupons with which each of us had been issued on arrival, stood in the long queue. As I peered at Jürgen through a gap between the two people dawdling ahead of me, I was suddenly overcome. How beautiful he was, with his broad shoulders, narrow waist, sunburned, scrupulously kept hands, and that wide fore-head above blue-green eyes set at an almost oriental angle under thick, arched brows! I had never before thought of a man as being beautiful. But beautiful was the only adjective to describe him. In comparison every other man and woman in the cafeteria seemed commonplace.

Jutta had moved ahead of Sally and me, to push her way vigorously through the crowd to Jürgen's table. When he saw her, he didn't get up for her, but merely pointed at another table where three more chairs stood vacant. Obediently, Jutta crossed over and hefted first one of the chairs and then another. I rushed to her. 'Let me carry one of those!'

Jutta struggled on, a chair under either fragile arm. 'No, no, Michael. No need. They are very light. But bring the other one.'

'You should have fetched those, Jürgen,' Sally said. 'Not left it to Jutta.'

Jürgen grinned, as though at a joke.

'It's all right, Sally.' Jutta set down the chairs. 'Jürgen has swum very much this afternoon. He is tired, I expect.'

Jürgen did not contradict her.

When Mervyn returned to the table, he was carrying only two tankards. He stared at Jutta, Sally and me, as though we were the last people he'd expected to be there. 'Oh, God!'

Jutta leapt to her feet. 'Never mind! I will get beer for us.'

I hurried after her. But 'No, no!' she cried, turning to push me away. 'Go back. I will fetch!'

'Really, Mervyn!' Sally chided him.

Mervyn carefully set down one tankard before Jürgen and the other before the chair that he himself was about to occupy. 'You women must be more logical.'

'Logical?'

'At the university you've now achieved the same status as men. Yes? Well, in that case, you shouldn't demand another kind of status as soon as there's anything difficult or tiresome to be done. Am I right, Jürgen?'

Jürgen smiled not at Mervyn but at me. 'You are perfectly right, Mervyn.'

'You carried Sally's luggage when we arrived,' I reminded him. 'You insisted.'

'If I remember correctly, I also carried Mervyn's. That was because both Sally and Mervyn were foreigners and guests.

'But surely, in similar circumstances, you'd carry Jutta's luggage?'

'Perhaps.' Jürgen laughed, tossing back his head. 'Or perhaps not. It would depend.'

'On what would it depend?'

'On what I thought about her at the moment.'

Suddenly I felt discouraged and tired. I couldn't be

bothered to argue any further.

Jutta returned with five tankards on a tin tray. 'There!' As she lowered one of the tankards, she splashed some of the beer on to Mervyn's slacks.

'Oh, Jutta, Jutta! What a clumsy girl!' Mervyn began to mop himself with a handkerchief.

'Sorry, sorry!' Jutta was abject. 'I brought five because I thought you and Jürgen will soon want some more and the line is so long.'

I drew a tankard towards me. 'You shouldn't spoil them, Jutta.'

'Thank you, Jutta.' Jürgen raised the fresh tankard set down before him, even though he'd not yet drained the other. '*Prosit!*' he said, looking only at her. Jutta gave him a radiant smile. Then he turned to me: 'You say that Jutta should not spoil us. But all her life Jutta has spoiled men. She can do nothing else. It is a habit. Yes, Jutta?'

Edging herself on to her chair, Jutta again smiled and nodded her head, as though in acknowledgement of a compliment.

'Well, what did you think of clever Eric's "discourse"?' Once again Mervyn put the word into mocking inverted commas. The question was for Jürgen.

Jürgen shrugged and then pulled a face.

'No, I didn't think you'd like it. I didn't think any of the Germans would like it.'

'I didn't like it either,' I said. 'He's supposed to be so brilliant and yet all he had to say was so banal.'

'Really, Michael? So that's your opinion? Well, you always were a sentimentalist, weren't you?' Mervyn put a finger in the small puddle of beer on the table between him and Jutta, and elongated it first in one direction and then in another until it made a rough star. 'Of course Eric has that ghastly Wykehamist manner and voice, as though he were speaking to cretins. And he's got an unerring knack for hitting on a cliché. But, you know, he talked sense.'

'He talked rubbish.'

'No, Michael, he did *not* talk rubbish. What he said was the truth – or as near to the truth as makes no difference. The Weimar Republic *was* an aberration – a kind of a caricature of a liberal democracy, invented by a people who had no real idea of what a liberal democracy was but had read about it in other countries and did their best to produce a copy. Jürgen?'

Jürgen, his head turned to gaze at another table, might not have heard.

'Jürgen, am I right or wrong?'

Jürgen now swivelled round to gaze at Mervyn. I could see the clenched muscles of the jaw closest to me, and the colour that had risen in the cheekbone above it. 'No, you are not right, my dear Mervyn. You are not right. In fact – if Sally and Jutta will pardon me for using the expression – you are talking – how do you say? – balls.'

Delighted, Mervyn threw back his head and burst into peal after peal of laughter. 'Oh, Jürgen, marvellous! Well done! Where on earth did you hear that expression?'

Now Jürgen, his fury gone, was also laughing. 'From you. From you! Don't you remember? You told me that you think *The Magic Mountain* balls, and I had no idea what you meant. I asked you to explain.'

'Yes, yes, I remember now, of course I remember.'

Jutta was looking uncomprehendingly, like a child among adults, from one face to another. 'I do not understand. Balls?' She turned to me for elucidation.

I told her crossly: 'Forget it, Jutta.' Then I leaned forward, putting a hand on her forearm: 'What did *you* think of what Eric had to say?'

Jutta gave a short, embarrassed laugh. 'I am sorry. I am ashamed. I slept!'

142

'Good for you. One should always sleep when people are talking balls.'

Mervyn rose. 'Another, Jürgen?'

'Why not?'

Mervyn slouched off. I stared after him, angrily wondering if his exclusion of the rest of us had been deliberate. Yes, I eventually decided, it had. From time to time, when he had seen too much of people, he would display this kind of ugliness.

Sally got to her feet. 'Jutta, I want a shower before we eat. I think I'll start back for home.'

Jutta darted a nervous glance at Jürgen. 'Do you wish me to come with you?' All too clearly she wished to remain.

'No, Jutta, of course not. Stay on here for a bit.'

Jutta's anxious frown cleared. 'I will not be long,' she compromised.

But Jürgen was also getting up. 'I, too must go. I have someone to see.' As always, he did not specify who this someone was.

Jutta put the question that I dared not put. 'Who is this someone?'

Jürgen smiled. 'No one you know.' He turned to me. 'You may drink my beer,' he said.

He went out by a different door from that taken by Sally.

XIV

The day before we left, we were to make an expedition. To Rosenheim. I had never before heard of the town. I was never to forget it.

For me the first mention of it was beside the river. Jürgen and Mervyn were arm-wrestling together, and of course it was Jürgen – so much stronger and so much more competitive, as though willing himself to avenge the defeat of his country in the war – who was always the winner. The lean, pale, wiry German whom everyone called Jo and who had been the chairman when Eric Friend had delivered his 'discourse', all at once jumped to his feet, his wet bathing costume sticking to his bony haunches, and clapped his hands for silence. Ignoring him, Jürgen and Mervyn continued to sway from side to side on the grass, grunting and screwing up their eyes with the effort of their contest. Jo squinted down at them with annoyance. Then, deciding to leave them to it, he said: 'You know that tomorrow we shall make an expedition, yes?'

'Yes, yes!' the dozen or so English students, led by Jessica, shouted back at him.

'We have no more speeches, no more discussions. Speeches and discussions are over.'

'Good show!' Harry shouted, to be applauded by the others.

'Edna has told me that in English you have a saying "All work and no play makes Jack a dull person."'

'A dull boy,' Edna corrected, adjusting a strap of her bathing-suit. Her body was glistening with the oil with

144

which, each time that she sunbathed, it had now become the task of Jeremy to smear her.

'A dull boy,' Jo repeated, clearly not liking to be put right. 'Well, tomorrow we take you to Rosenheim. This is Jürgen's idea. He has made the plans.'

'Three cheers for Jürgen!' Harry cried out.

'Have you heard of Rosenheim?' Jo asked.

'Of course,' Eric Friend answered, while the rest of the English shook their heads and shouted out 'No! No!'

Having finished yet another arm-wrestling match, Jürgen now leapt to his feet and raced across to Jo, throwing an arm about his bare shoulders. The contrast between the physiques of the two men was cruel. 'Since this is my idea, I will explain to you. Rosenheim is one of the finest centres of German Romanesque architecture.'

'German *what*?' a female English voice demanded, to be followed by 'Come again!' from another male one.

'Oh, for God's sake shut up and don't display your ignorance!' Although Mervyn wasn't joking, the students at whom he'd shouted fortunately thought that he was. There were cries, in mock upper-class accents, of 'Oh, I say!' and hoots of good-natured derision.

Jürgen continued: 'Rosenheim contains one of the most beautiful cathedrals in Germany, perhaps in the whole world.'

'Yes, in the whole world!' Jo interjected.

'There is also another basilica, almost as beautiful. It is called St Michael's. It was built in the eleventh century after Christ. Its founder was St Bernard.'

'Who ever heard of a basilica founded by a dog?' Jeremy put in.

'Oh, shut up!' Jessica shouted at him.

Jürgen paid no attention. 'There are many beautiful churches, museums, houses. I think that you will enjoy your visit. Yes, I know that you will.'

'This evening,' Jo said, 'we shall show you some pictures of Rosenheim and Jürgen here will speak some
more about it.'

'Yes, we have some slides. This is not the place nor the
time to give you a lecture, but please, if you are interested,
come to the lecture room at eight o'clock tonight.'

Jürgen now crossed over to squat beside me, his hands
dangling between his bare knees. My mouth all at once
felt dry. I was conscious of the beating of my heart, a
painful thudding within me.

'You have really never heard of Rosenheim?'

'Never.'

He shook his head in disbelief. 'Incredible! It is as
though I have never heard of Canterbury.' Then his body
tilted closer. 'On the bus you will sit next to me. Will you
do that?'

'Of course, Jürgen!' I laughed with pleasure.

'Good.' Leaning forward, he patted my left hand with
his right. Then he gave me a conspiratorial wink, before
he jumped up and hurried away from me.

XV

That morning all of us, the Germans no less than the English, were behaving like small children just emerged from school. There was a lot of shouting, laughter and horseplay as, in pairs or small groups, rucksacks on backs or hold-alls dangling from hands, we gradually assembled beside the three charabancs – or 'charas', as Jutta, with her extraordinary gift for mimicry called them, after having heard Jeremy once use the word – parked in a gleaming line in the university square. The drivers, young men in military-looking khaki trousers and khaki shirts, with short-cut hair as glossy with the German equivalent of Brylcreem as their brown shoes were shiny with polish, looked so alike that they might have been brothers. They stood, each outside his bus, in a posture, legs apart and hands clasped behind back, that reinforced the impression of soldiers on parade.

I pushed impatiently through the crowds, with Jutta struggling along behind me. I had gone over to her lodgings, having heard that Sally was ill. Then, leaving Sally behind with yet another paperback detective-story – she seemed to have nothing worse than a stomach upset – we had come on together. A young German, whose name I couldn't remember, grabbed at my arm. 'Michael! You will sit with me, yes?' I smiled vaguely at him and pulled myself free. 'Sorry, I've already promised ... '

'Have you seen Edna?' Jeremy hurried up to ask. 'She said she'd meet me here at quarter to, and there's not a sign of her.'

''Fraid not,' I replied over a shoulder, still hurrying on.

I began to peer into the first of the buses, already half filled with people. No sign of Jürgen! The straps of the hold-all that I was carrying for Jutta – it contained the sandwiches that she had prepared for us early that morning – was biting deep into my palm. Although it was not yet ten o'clock, I could feel the sweat on my forehead and under my arms.

'Why don't we sit in here?' Jutta asked, panting behind, her thin body bowed under the rucksack that contained further provisions.

'I'm looking for the others.' There was no need for me to say which others I meant.

'Perhaps they have not yet arrived. There are more people than seats, I think. Some will have to stand. We do not wish to stand, do we? Let us sit somewhere quickly, yes?'

Paying no attention to her, I now began to edge my way through the crowd beside the second of the chara-bancs. For a moment I thought that I saw Jürgen's head and my heart lifted. Then I realised that it was someone else – a student with a limp from a war-wound. He was of the same height as Jürgen, he had the same muscular physique, his eyes had the same kind of oriental slant above high cheekbones. But whereas everyone, male or female, always looked at Jürgen, mysteriously no one ever gave this other German more than an indifferent glance.

I arrived at the third bus. It was less full than the other two, perhaps because to reach it involved the longest walk. As though touting for custom, the driver smiled at me cheerfully and indicated the door beside him with a bow. '*Bitte, bitte!*'

I returned his smile, shook my head, and continued

148

along the charabanc, peering into each window in turn. Then I saw Jürgen – in the last seat of all, a newspaper supported on the back of the seat ahead of him and his head lowered to read it. Eagerly, I raised a hand and tapped on the window. Paying no attention, Jürgen went on reading. It was only then that I realised that the seat beside him was occupied by Mervyn – who was gazing into space as he picked between his front teeth with what appeared to be a bus ticket. I felt a spasm of anger, intense but transient, like a nauseous churning of the gut. But probably he was only sitting there to keep Jürgen company until my arrival. Yes, that must be it, of course that must be it.

'There they are!' Jutta now squealed behind me, raising an arm to point.

'Yes, I've already seen them.' I rapped more violently on the window. But still neither looked round. I rapped again. This time Jürgen lowered the newspaper, slowly turned his head, and at last looked at me. He stared. He might have been staring with vague interrogation at some stranger about to ask for directions. Beyond him, Mervyn was craning round to see who it was. Then, with far more enthusiasm than Jürgen, he waved an arm. So morose for the last two days – clearly he had had enough of both Germany and the conference – he now looked jolly and relaxed.

I went back to the door of the charabanc and clambered aboard. Jutta followed me. From time to time the hold-all struck against the legs of people already seated and then I cried out 'Sorry, sorry!'

'Jürgen! Here we are!' I was breathless.

'There you are!' Then, as I stood beside the seat, expecting him to ask Mervyn to move to another, he pointed to the luggage rack: 'Put your bag up there. It will be more comfortable for you if you do not have it on your knees all through the journey.' At that, he raised the newspaper again and was once more absorbed.

'Hello, Jutta.' Mervyn's greeting was cheerful.

'Hello, Mervyn.' Jutta was struggling with the straps of her rucksack.

'Let me help you,' I said.

'Always the perfect little gentleman.'

'Unlike you, Mervyn. You're just a tike.'

Our banter was good-humoured.

Jürgen looked at his watch. 'We are late to start. What are they doing?' He got up, squeezed past Mervyn's knees, and made his way down the aisle to the door. Leaning out from it, he shouted to the people outside, who then began to clamber aboard.

Jeremy's face appeared. 'Where's Edna? Anyone seen Edna?'

'Perhaps she's gone off on a private excursion with Duffy,' Mervyn shouted down the bus.

Jeremy either did not hear the remark or decided to ignore it. 'Edna! Edna!' he called, as though she might have hidden herself under one of the seats or in one of the luggage racks.

'No point in waiting for her. We are too late already.' Jürgen seized Jeremy by the arm and dragged him off the steps into the interior, as though he were a dummy. But now, standing in the aisle so that people even later than himself had to squeeze past him, Jeremy continued to bleat 'Edna, Edna, Edna!' as he searched the seats all around.

'Sit!' Jürgen ordered.

The first bus and then the second pulled out. The engine of our own wheezed asthmatically – was it going to refuse to start? – before it coughed into life.

As the driver released the handbrake, Jeremy, who was still standing despite Jürgen's peremptory order, all at once wailed in anguish: 'There! There! There she is!'

Looking back over my shoulder through the rear-window, I could see Edna at the opposite end of the square from the direction in which we were moving. Dressed in a pale-pink coat and skirt, she was running, legs helter-skelter, on heels even higher than those that she'd worn at the picnic, in pursuit of the retreating bus.

Jürgen, still standing like Jeremy, had also seen her. He leaned forward and said something in German to the driver, who, instead of braking, then accelerated.

'Stop! Stop!' Jeremy screamed. 'Can't you see? She's there! There!' The bus gathered momentum. 'Oh, you clot! Can't you *see*?' He pushed past Jürgen, leaned over and slapped the driver on the shoulder. '*Nein! Nein! Stopfen! Stopfen!*'

The Germans began to laugh, and one of them, a girl, called out in imitation: '*Stopfen! Stopfen!*'

Again looking back, I could see Edna standing disconsolately in the middle of the square, her straw hat in one hand and her handbag in the other, as she gazed after the charabanc.

Then, all at once, the driver had given a wrench to the wheel, and the charabanc was wheeling around in a circle. Jürgen began to laugh, and once again, as at the '*Stopfen, stopfen!*', the Germans took up the laughter. About both Jürgen's laughter and theirs, there was something savage and vindictive.

The charabanc now drove towards Edna at such speed that I thought for a moment that, paralysed by its onrush, she would allow it to run her over. Then the driver slammed on the brakes and the bus squealed to halt. Everyone, English and German, burst into spontaneous clapping. The driver, grinning, pulled at a handle to open the door. Once more there was clapping as Edna, with Jeremy rushing forward to hand her up, teetered aboard.

'Did you really think we would leave you behind, Edna?' Jürgen asked.

It was obvious, from the view that I'd had of that solitary figure standing disconsolate in the middle of the empty square, that Edna had thought it. But now, as she sank down into a seat next to Jeremy and opened her bag to take out a handkerchief with which to dab at her face, she shook her head gamely: 'Of course not! I knew it was just another of your Germanic little jokes.'

'Germanic? And how does a Germanic little joke differ from an English little one?'

Edna laughed. 'When we've spent most of the past two weeks talking rubbish about national characteristics, do we want to talk more rubbish about them on an outing?'

I admired her spirit.

Jeremy fumbled in a pocket of his shorts, pulled out a Naafi toffee and offered it to her. Wrinkling up her nose, she shrugged it away, without a word.

'Sure?'

She didn't answer.

Jürgen put out a hand. 'I will have it.'

Reluctantly Jeremy yielded it to him. Jürgen then made his way, hand to the rail to steady himself, down the aisle to his seat next to Mervyn.

'Oh, Jürgen! What a cruel trick! You should have seen the anguish on poor Jeremy's face.' Mervyn's tone was congratulatory, not disapproving.

'And the anguish on Edna's,' I put in angrily.

'I saw both,' Jürgen said. 'Since relief is probably the most enjoyable of all human emotions, one should not refuse to pay for it with anguish. Yes?'

There was a silence among the four of us, while the other passengers chatted noisily. Then Jutta turned to me: 'Once this countryside was very beautiful. Trees,

152

flowers, green fields. Old houses. But the bombing was terrible.'

'Saturation bombing,' came Jürgen's voice from behind. 'That is the right phrase?'

'Absolutely right,' Mervyn confirmed.

'In a few years perhaps everything will become as it was. But now ... ' Jutta looked forlorn, as she gazed out of the window at the dun landscape, stretching away to the line, wavering in a heat-haze, of the distant horizon. Trees had been jaggedly amputated or totally uprooted from the reddish loam. Bomb craters, filled in with rubble and soil, pocked the road, so that the driver was constantly obliged to swerve in his often unsuccessful attempts to prevent the charabanc from bumping across them.

'There are no leaves, no leaves anywhere.' I was overcome by the flat, endless dreariness. 'And not a bush, not a single bush.'

'No leaves ... Not a single bush,' Jutta echoed. Her face seemed to have acquired the dusty greyness of the road over which we were heaving and bucking. Her voice fell away as though she were speaking out of some deep pit of exhaustion and grief. Seemingly no less oppressed, all the other students, previously so noisy as they had shouted across the aisles to each other, had now fallen silent.

'Have we far to go?' Mervyn asked Jürgen.

'It was not so far when the road was good. But now ... '

'Ah, well, I suppose Rosenheim will make it all worthwhile.'

'Yes, Rosenheim will make it all worthwhile.'

The sound of Jutta clearing her throat – dust was whirling through the window beside her – might almost have been a whimper.

Eventually, I slept. Jutta slept beside me, her head on my shoulder, with her soft, wispy, reddish-brown hair – it might have been a baby's – brushing my cheek. From time to time, through a dream of swimming with Jürgen on and on down the river, under now overhanging willows and now a sky of clearest blue, I'd be conscious of her twitching nervously against me, like some high-strung animal. Then my sleep deepened until total oblivion engulfed me.

'Michael! Michael! Wake up! Wake up!' Jürgen's palm was on my shoulder, shaking me. English voices were exclaiming in surprise all around. Hands reached up for rucksacks and bags, bodies struggled towards the exit.

'Oh! Have we arrived?'

'We have arrived.'

I yawned and swallowed on the sour taste in my mouth. Jutta was hauling herself up, her hand on the seat in front. 'I will get down our things.'

'No, leave them! I'll see to them!'

But Jutta squeezed past me, to reach for the rucksack and hold-all. After that the four of us joined the shuffling queue to descend.

Mervyn was the first of us to do so. Then, suddenly gallant, he held out his hands for Jutta to jump.

The crowds began to clear around the buses. I looked about me. In amazement, I asked: 'Where are we? What is this?'

Mervyn answered: 'This, Michael, is Rosenheim.' There was suppressed anger in his voice.

'*This?*'

'Yes, this is Rosenheim.' Jürgen sounded buoyant, as though at some secret joke on the point of being divulged.

Before my London school had been evacuated, my father had once taken me, in the early days of the Blitz, on a visit to my widowed grandmother in her house, later to be destroyed by a fire-bomb, high above Greenwich. His object was to persuade her to move with us into safety, but with peevish obstinacy – there was, in fact, nothing of importance to keep her there – she'd refused. On the journey by car – as a doctor, my father received a special allowance of petrol, which he wasn't entirely scrupulous about using only for visits to his patients – I'd stared out in horror at the results of the Blitz on a part of London I'd rarely even seen. Walls had collapsed, to reveal giant, dilapidated dolls' houses, in which blackened clothes still hung in half-open wardrobes, pots still rested on kitchen-ranges exposed to the open sky, and bedclothes still trailed in squalid disarray from beds that would never now be made. Limbs of trees had been fractured, their splintered bones sticking through greenish-white bark. There were holes in the roads, fenced off and covered with tarpaulin. There were grimy men at work in boiler-suits and gum-boots. There were knots of laughing, indomitable women, weighted down with shopping-bags. There were boisterous children, not much younger than myself, playing hopscotch on the cement-paved area in front of a wrecked tenement building.

Now starkly, as I stood in front of the bus gazing about me, this memory returned. What I had seen on that afternoon in South London had been terrible. But what I now saw about me was even more so. Hardly a house in this quarter stood intact. Later we were to pass through another where, mercifully, some of the oldest houses had been spared. Where roofs had been sliced off or bashed in, emergency bandages of tarpaulin had been applied. Wounds in the façades of once noble houses had been patched with corrugated iron, already gritty with rust. There were blackened trees, blackened stones, even the cobbles were blackened, where they had not been shattered and scattered.

The strange thing was that the people who lived in these once beautiful and now ruined houses, like troglodytes in underground gloom, all looked clean and neat as they went about their business. As in Hildingen, many of them halted to stare at us newcomers when they heard our foreign voices and saw our foreign faces and clothes. What were they feeling? Resentment, anger, bafflement, amazement, envy? As in Hildingen, it was impossible to guess.

Edna, beside me now, gave a little shudder despite the noonday heat. 'One can *smell* the fires, can't one?'

'Yes.' I'd already begun to feel nauseated by the reek of charred wood and – I had somehow dottily convinced myself – also of charred flesh.

Jürgen jumped up on to what could still be recognised as having been a drinking trough, even if its basin now lay upside down, in three jagged fragments, beside its cracked granite base. Dominating us, as a heroic statue on its plinth dominates a square, he clapped his hands for silence. 'This is Rosenheim!' he announced, as though some of us might still think otherwise. 'It is perhaps not entirely what you expected but I think that we have an – an interesting experience for you all here. Yes? I certainly hope so. Now – if you will be so kind, will you all follow me?'

As he looked down at our upturned faces, one of the English, I couldn't see who, shouted out an ironic '*Jawohl, mein Führer!*'

At that there were nervous giggles from people clearly as unnerved as I by the totally unexpected destruction all about us.

Jürgen continued: 'If you get lost, the buses will leave the square here – or what is left of the square here – at

156

six o'clock.' He repeated it slowly, as though for a group of small children: 'Six o'clock. Six o'clock. From this square. Those who are not here by six o'clock will have to make their own way back to Hildingen, and that may not be easy. Do you understand?' He looked around the faces. 'Edna?'

Edna, accepting the role of schoolchild, held up a hand. 'I won't be late this time. Guide's honour.'

Interminably we trailed from one bombed building to another, with Jürgen lecturing us. This had been a fifteenth-century house, built by a cloth-merchant and most recently occupied by a well-known lawyer, who had been killed in it along with his wife, his wife's mother and his three children. This was the ruin, no more than the apse and a side-chapel, of one of the most beautiful of all the churches. This was the Cathedral, of which we had seen photographs the night before. Fortunately the bronze doors and chandeliers, stored away in the Harz mountains at the outbreak of the war, had survived. This had been a hospital. As we could see, it was a modern building, of no architectural interest, ugly even. But many doctors and nurses had been killed, many patients too, of course.

As we made this tour, I soon realised that the German students were spending far more time examining the horrified or uneasy faces of their guests than the buildings or artefacts about which Jürgen spoke. There was something eerie, even menacing, about this constant scrutiny.

Mervyn was now beside me. As we trekked up a hill towards the carbon-encrusted ruin of what looked like yet another church, he at last broke the gloomy silence. 'It was a good joke, really. Wasn't it? I mean the joke about this bomb-site, not about abandoning poor Edna. Typical of Jürgen. Of all this dim shower, only he could have thought of it. Yes, I like it. Now it's our turn for

157

punishment. All these days we've been telling them of all their iniquities and now – hey presto! – they're showing us one of ours.'

'But are they comparable? What they did was so much worse. If one paraded them round Stalingrad – or round a concentration camp . . .' I broke off. Once again I hadn't the heart for this terrible arithmetic of balancing disaster against disaster, atrocity against atrocity, death against death.

'One has to hand it to Jürgen,' Mervyn went on, beginning to puff as we strode on and on up the hill at the hectic pace set by Jürgen.

'Oh, yes! Of course!' Suddenly I felt angry.

Even more breathless than we were, her straw hat pulled down low over her forehead and her crocodile-leather handbag swinging, Edna now overtook us, with Jeremy in pursuit. 'Oh, I'm so hungry!' she wailed. 'When do you think we're going to go back to eat our food?'

In order not to have to lug them around with us, we'd left our rucksacks and bags in a café that was little more than a hole in a half-collapsed wall, with chairs and tables set out before it.

'Not for a long, long time, would be my guess,' Mervyn told her.

'I should have jumped at Duffy's offer to take me for a drive instead. What a fool I was!'

As we at last neared the summit of the hill, Edna clutching on to Jeremy's arm so as not to topple over on the cobbles, we could hear Jürgen once again holding forth: 'You may remember that I showed you pictures of an art gallery. This was the art gallery. Yes, this! The entrance was here.' He pointed to a half-collapsed arch. 'And here, just here . . .'

Not for the first time during the tour, I allowed my

attention to wander. From a house that was no more than a crushed shell patched up with corrugated iron and tarpaulins, an elderly woman, dressed all in black, had emerged. She was dragging behind her the kind of broom that a witch in a Grimm's fairy-tale might use for her flights. Vigorously she set about sweeping first the three chunks of concrete masonry that did service for her steps, turning the brush now this way and now that to get its bristles into the crevices, and then the cracked area of pavement beyond them. There was grim, unrelenting determination in the regular movements of her thin arms. Her fingers, crooked with arthritis, gripped the broomhandle so fiercely that their joints showed white. Eventually having become conscious of my scrutiny, she raised her head to stare across at me with what seemed hostility, even hatred, in eyes narrowed to slits under a screwed-up bun of white hair. Then, with a shrug, she returned to her labours.

Jürgen was announcing: 'Now we shall walk back to the café to eat.' He grinned impudently at us. 'If you are hungry, that is.' He looked at his watch, prompting me to look at mine. It was already past two.

'*If* we are hungry!' Jeremy exclaimed, at the same moment as Edna cried out: 'Oh, goody gumdrops! I'm absolutely famished! I could eat a horse, even an elephant.'

'To judge from the look of the sandwiches that Frau Kassel has made for us, I shouldn't be surprised if it isn't a horse that we shall be eating.' Jeremy had undertaken to see to the food for himself and Edna.

'Oh, why, why, why did I let you be responsible for our food?'

Jürgen, having relinquished his role of guide, joined Mervyn and me on our descent of the hill. As though determined to woo us back after having alienated us with his brutal joke, he put one arm round Mervyn's shoulders and the other round mine. 'Have I tired you? Have I kept you waiting too long for your food?'

'The answer to both of those questions is yes. I've a blister on my heel, and Michael's going to faint if he doesn't tuck into something soon.'

Jürgen squeezed our shoulders. 'I love this town.'

'Wouldn't it be more correct to say "I loved this town" – in the past tense?'

'No, Mervyn. I love it – present tense. I love it still. I can see it as it was and I can see it as it will be again. Yes, wait, wait and see!' He turned to me: 'You do not feel that about your London?'

'There's still so much of London left.'

'In some places too much,' Mervyn added. 'Ugly, squalid things that would have been better smashed or incinerated.'

'With all the people inside them?' I asked.

Again Jürgen squeezed our shoulders. I could feel his pectoral muscles hardening against my arm. 'I am sad,' he said. 'Sad about Rosenheim. Sad about London. Sad about this terrible war that made such destruction possible. Also I am sad for another, more personal reason. Tomorrow Mervyn, Michael and Sally – dear friends – will leave for England.'

'We'll meet again,' I said, silently willing that to be true.

'Of course we'll meet again,' Mervyn seconded.

I went on: 'You must come and stay with us. And you don't have to worry about currency. You've been so kind to us – done so much for us – here.'

Jürgen flashed me a smile. Then his mood of happy affection all at once changed: 'Do you really want another German in England when you still have all those prisoners of war?' The tone was harsh, aggressive. He dropped his arms from our shoulders. 'Aren't the mother and father of one of those prisoners coming to see you this evening, Mervyn?'

'Yep, that's right.' In Oxford, Mervyn had befriended a group of prisoners of war from a nearby camp at Headington, entertaining them to tea in his rooms, when he would play them music on his gramophone or talk to them in German. Occasionally, I'd also ask them round. 'Heinrich – one of my Germans – asked me to see them. I have some photographs from him – and a food-parcel.'

'Is this food-parcel from him or from you?' Jürgen's tone was still harsh.

'From me. Those prisoners don't get enough food to spare any. But he's made something for his parents – I don't know what it is.'

'You have not looked to see?'

'No, I haven't unwrapped the parcel. The Customs didn't ask me to do so.'

Suddenly, Jürgen was once more friendly. His arms returned to our shoulders. 'He is lucky, this Heinrich, to have you for a friend. I can see that.'

'I'm lucky to have him for a friend.'

'A good German?'

'Yes, a good German – like many Germans. Perhaps most Germans.'

There were so few tables and chairs outside the little café that the late-comers had to squat on the grass. The sky had darkened and acquired a coppery sheen, the air was heavy. Flies settled on food, faces and bare arms and legs. Jutta had raced down the hill and 'bagged' – she herself used the word, another picked up from the English – a table and some chairs, fending off any invader with 'Sorry! Sorry!' in English or, more peremptorily, *'Nein, nein!'* in German.

Mervyn opened the first sandwich offered to him and

161

peered inside it at the thick slices of liver sausage, pink marbled with white. He plucked off the chunk of pickled gherkin resting on top and threw it away from him, pulling a disgusted face.

I laughed. 'I'm sorry you think so little of Jutta's sandwiches.'

'One can't blame the cook for the ingredients.' He bit into the sandwich and began to munch. 'I always think of this bread' – he held up the sandwich into which he had bitten – 'as utility bread. The gastronomic equivalent of utility furniture. It's the same depressing shade of beige, and it has almost the same texture.'

I was embarrassed by his tactlessness, as I'd so often been in the course of the trip. 'At least you won't have to eat it for much longer, as our friends here will.'

'True, true.'

Jürgen prised open a bottle of beer with the all-purpose Swiss penknife that he always carried around with him. He'd brought a number of tin cups, one inside the other. He poured out beer into one and then handed it not to Jutta or to me but to Mervyn. 'You must tell us what is the furniture equivalent of this beer,' he told him drily.

At that he suffered another abrupt change of mood. Jumping to his feet, he began to pour beer into the remaining tin cups with such haste and vigour that it foamed up over the rims. 'Come! Come! Let us drink a toast!' He handed round the cups, then raised his own, the sunlight that had suddenly filtered through a leaden cloud glinting on it. 'Ladies and gentlemen – to Anglo-German friendship!'

Jutta now jumped to her feet. 'To friendship through the whole world!'

To my amazement, Mervyn now also sprang up, his cup raised high. 'To everlasting peace!' He said it without any of his customary irony.

All the other people at our table shuffled to their feet, cups raised, to be followed, at first sporadically and then in larger and larger numbers, by the groups, whether at other tables or on the grass, all around us.

'Say the toast again, Mervyn!' Edna cried out, her face flushed as though from too much beer, even though she'd so far taken only a sip. 'Say the toast again! Again!'

'Yes, again, again!' other English voices took up.

Mervyn clambered up on to his chair. It swayed perilously, until I put out a hand to steady it. He raised his glass high. Then, in a loud, passionate voice, totally unlike his usually soft and contained one, he cried out: 'Ladies and gentlemen, *meine Herren, meine Damen!* Let me ask all of you to drink with us to Anglo-German friendship in particular and to universal friendship in general. Let us drink to those two things and to world peace!'

Raggedly the others took up the last words: 'World peace, world peace!'

Suddenly self-conscious, Mervyn descended from the chair, to have Jürgen throw his arms about him and kiss him on either cheek. '*Brüder, brüder!*' I heard him exclaim as he did so. Then Jutta, setting down her cup in such haste that it tipped over, beer frothing from it, also threw her arms round Mervyn, similarly pressing her lips first to one cheek and then the other.

After this, looking even more self-conscious, Mervyn seated himself. His passion and vehemence had clearly taken him as much by surprise as it had taken me.

When we had finished our picnic, we sat on for a long time, under the heavy, coppery sky, talking and, many of us, smoking. The offering and acceptance of cigarettes, like the offering and acceptance of beer, had by then become for us a symbol of the offering and acceptance of the friendship that Mervyn had just toasted.

'Have one of these?'

'What are they?'

'Players.'

'Ah, Players! Players are good, very good, But first you must have a German cigarette. German cigarettes are not so good now. But you must try a German cigarette.'

'H'm. Not at all bad.'

'You like the German cigarette?'

'Yes. Yes, I do.'

It seemed as if throughout our visit I'd heard this conversation or one very like it over and over again.

Eventually Jürgen rose and called for silence. 'There is one more thing to show you.' From around him, not merely from us English but also from the Germans, there came groans. 'No, you must come.' He was serious, not joking. 'This is important. This is something you must see before you leave Rosenheim. Yes, please!' He made a gesture to us with both his hands, like a conductor telling his orchestra to take a bow. 'Come!'

Wearily I rose, as everyone around me was doing.

'You may again leave in the café what you do not wish to carry. Everything will be safe.'

'Of course it will be safe,' Mervyn said to me in a sarcastic undertone. 'The Germans are so honest.'

'Well, they are,' Edna protested, having overheard him. 'And when many of them are homeless and there's precious little to eat – well, honesty's not all that easy, I'd have thought. Look at all those stories coming out of Italy.'

'We seem to be going back to the Cathedral!' Jeremy cried out in anguish. 'I can't go there again – not if Jürgen's going to repeat his lecture! Jürgen! Jürgen!' He raced ahead to catch up with Jürgen and three other Germans leading the already straggling procession.

'Jürgen!' He grabbed hold of his arm. 'Are you taking us back to the Cathedral?'

Jürgen halted, smiling. 'Yes. We are returning to the Cathedral.'

Others of the English had now also caught up with them. 'But why? Why? Why?' they began to ask.

'Because there is something there that I have not yet shown to you. I have kept it to the last for you. It is important that it comes at the end. You will see. It will be interesting for you.'

'What's he talking about?' Edna demanded.

Mervyn was resigned, turning away with a shrug of the shoulders. 'Search me. The ways of Jürgen are like the ways of God.'

The once noisy and energetic but now silent and listless crocodile wound down a rough path, tussocks of grass pushing up here and there, to the desolate ruin, open to the sky, of the vast cathedral. Previously, we'd taken another route, along a main road. The charred smell, omnipresent in the town, had now become particularly strong. On our earlier visit, Jürgen had marched us up the deserted aisle to a pit covered over with tarpaulin and had then pointed, with what had struck me as a flourish of pride: 'The altar – one of the most beautiful in Europe – used to be here.' But now, instead of walking through the ruins, he conducted us around them, until he brought us up short at a clearing where two benches, clearly new, faced each other. Between the benches there was a well-kept flower-bed, and behind one of them the vestiges of a wall, its highest section covered with what, at first sight, seemed to be a dead briar rose, its stock blackened with fire.

Jürgen pointed at the wall. 'The cloisters were here.' Looking around me, I'd already made out the broken stones of what must once have been a fountain. 'This

165

rose was already here in 815 – that is more than a thousand years ago – when Louis the Debonair' – 'Who? Who? Who was he?' English voices asked, to receive no answer – 'hid his belongings under it. The next day the belongings were missing. You might have supposed that Louis would have decided that that was a bad omen, but to him it was a good one. So it was here that he founded Rosenheim. When the Cathedral was destroyed with the bombing, the rose tree seemed to be dead. But last year' – he pointed up into the spidery, blackened branches – 'a shoot appeared. Look! Up there! You can all of you see it?'

The English clustered together and craned their necks. Jeremy, like a small child, stood first on tiptoe and then began to bounce up and down. Arm raised to point, he shouted out in triumph: 'Yes, yes! I can see it! Over there! Just over there!'

'Where, where, where?' the others asked. Then 'Oh, yes, yes, I see it!' Edna squealed, followed by two more of the English. Eventually everyone had seen it, myself included. High up in a blackened branch, there was a single straggly, yellowish-brown shoot, so sickly-looking that it seemed as if it would be a miracle if it ever survived the winter.

'Will it survive?' I asked. The others looked disapprovingly at me, as though this doubt might in itself jeopardise the rose's future.

'We believe so,' Jürgen said crisply, clearly annoyed with me for having put the question. Then he turned to Mervyn: 'Do you have such a rose tree in England?'

'We have many rose trees. Of course we do. But whether we have one as old as this one . . .'

'You do not understand me. What I wish to say is, do you have a rose tree that seemed to be dead for two, three years and then suddenly it came to life again?'

166

'I've no idea.'

The Germans had begun to argue vehemently among themselves. I turned to Jeremy, who was now standing beside me: 'What's all that about?'

'Search me! You know I don't understand a word of their gabble.'

Mervyn had now rejoined us. 'Mervyn – translate!'

Mervyn listened for a time to the hubbub. Then: 'Wonderfully Germanic. They're arguing about the species of that rose. That one over there' – he indicated a boy in *lederhosen*, with a coxcomb of carrot-coloured hair – 'says it's a *rosa centifolia*, but that one' – he indicated a busty girl with a round, shiny face – 'says it must be a *rosa gallica*. But that one' – he indicated a studious-looking boy, with whom I'd sometimes chatted – 'says it can't be a *rosa gallica* because *rosa gallica* grows only in the South of Europe.'

'Oh, Mervyn, you're making all this up!' Edna cried out.

'Not a bit of it. But I can see why you think I am.'

Eventually the argument among the German students petered out. Jürgen jumped up on to one of the benches and yet again clapped his hands for attention. 'So now you have seen our famous rose tree. I hope that our English friends will have found something symbolic in its rebirth. Most of us Germans do, yes?' He looked around among his fellow countrymen. Many of them nodded vigorously. 'Well, our guided tour has now ended.' There was a ragged cheer from some of the English, to which he made ironic acknowledgement with a stiff bow. 'Thank you. I hope that at least some of you have enjoyed it. The buses' – he looked at his watch – 'do not leave for another hour and seven minutes. We have finished our programme sooner than I expected. So now you are free, to do what you wish. There is a swimming-pool, unbombed. Also unbombed, there is a museum of Egyptian antiquities.' From the same section of the English as before, there came loud groans. 'Or you may, if that is what you prefer – and I think it is what many of our English friends prefer – do nothing. Jo will guide those who wish to go to the swimming-pool, and Siegfried here will guide those who wish to see the Egyptian antiquities.'

'The Egyptian antiquities are very fine,' Siegfried said encouragingly. But when he called 'Please! Please come with me, those who wish to come!' only the English twin sisters, always inseparable, went with him.

I crossed over to Jürgen. 'And what are you going to do?'

He turned and smiled. 'I am going to do nothing with you.' As he spoke the words, they struck me as strangely, even ominously ambiguous.

'And are you going to do nothing with me too?' Edna asked coquettishly.

Jürgen again smiled. 'I will do nothing with any of you. Or with all of you. As you wish it.' All those standing around him, about a dozen in number, looked perplexed. Then he said: 'Come! Let us go down the hill! We will go back to the café, yes?'

Walking towards the café, I was determined to keep with Jürgen. Mervyn, it was clear, was no less determined to keep with us. Having been so sternly pedagogic while leading us on the tour, Jürgen now began to behave like an irresponsible schoolboy. First he challenged Mervyn to a race from one corner to the next – a contest which, of course, he won. Then he ran into a children's playground, jumped on a seesaw and, in the manner of a tightrope walker, arms extended, teetered from one end to the other. Finally, when we came to an incline, he caught me by a hand and, shouting 'Run, run run!' dragged me with him to the bottom. Once there, he faced me, my hand still in his. 'You are so young, Michael. You are almost the youngest of everyone – younger than Jutta, or Mervyn, or me. Yet you always want to behave like someone older.'

'Do I?'

'Yes. Why, why?'

'I've no idea.'

We began to walk on.

'We have all had so much more experience than you. Jutta has had her terrible war experiences, and Mervyn was a soldier. And I ...' What precisely he had gone through he did not reveal. I wish now that I'd asked him. Instead, I said: 'What were Jutta's war experiences?'

In a suddenly hostile voice, he demanded: 'Why do you wish to know?'

'Why not?'

'You are not interested in Jutta.'

'Of course I'm interested in Jutta. I've come to think of her as a friend.'

He gave an abrupt, scornful laugh. Then he said: 'I will tell you, but you must not tell Jutta that I have told you. Her home is in the East, yes? She is working as an assistant in her father's pharmacy. The Russians enter the town. They force their way into the pharmacy. They take many things. When Jutta's father makes a protest, they kill him, shoot him. They shoot her mother also. They take Jutta and her sister away and then they do terrible things to them. Fuck them like animals. Many men, many times. Both have to work for the Russians. Slaves.'

As he told the story, his face grew dark and congested, like a sky before a storm.

He squinted angrily at me. 'Is that enough?'

'Enough?'

'Do you want more?' he asked, quietly savage. 'Then

perhaps you must ask Jutta.'

I felt a strange terror and disgust. With an effort I suppressed them.

'And how did she come to Hildingen?' I asked.

'How? She makes friends with a Russian officer. You understand? He fucks, fucks, fucks her. Then he helps her.'

'Horrible.' And I did genuinely feel it to be horrible. 'All those ruined lives.'

'Yes, all those ruined lives.' For a moment he was silent. Then again, he gave his abrupt, scornful laugh. 'And now you are here to punish us.'

'To punish you?' Suddenly I remembered what Mervyn had said about punishment only a short time before.

'Yes, of course, to punish us. What else? To tell us that we had been bad boys and girls to have allowed that Pied Piper of a Hitler to lead us astray, and to instruct us to be better in the future. That was how that colonel of yours – that, that Duffy – intended it to be. In his own way he punishes his secretary, and he planned for you to punish us.'

'No, Jürgen. No! I've never thought of it like that. And I'm sure Sally and Mervyn have never thought of it like that. We've come here as friends, not punishers.'

'Friends?' Then suddenly he relaxed. He smiled. 'Well, you have become friends. My first English friends.' He threw an arm round my shoulder and pulled me to him.

Although at this hour of late afternoon many of the café tables were unoccupied, most of our party now preferred to squat or lie out on the grass. Soon, with the restlessness that constantly moved through him like a fire, Jürgen was teaching us a German round. We were ranged in a circle about him, he squatted on his hunkers, from time to time jumping to his feet when he became impatient with our slowness. 'No, no, no, Michael! *Du, du* ... Your voice must go up a semitone, not down. Up! Yes, try it again, please.' Self-consciously I sang the phrase. 'Good, good!' He turned: 'Now, Edna! ... Ah, I love Edna's voice, even if, like Michael, she does not always sing in tune. Who would imagine that Edna would have such a deep, dark voice?'

When he thought we were all as near to perfect as he'd ever achieve, he jumped up on to a chair and began to conduct us, swaying from side to side, eyes shut and face contorted, in a parody of an exhibitionistic maestro. I burst into laughter: 'Idiot!' At that he tut-tutted at me, shaking his head in simulated anger.

When the time at last came for us to board the chara-banc, Jürgen touched my arm with unusual gentleness, the thumb and forefinger of his right hand holding it just above the elbow. 'Now you will sit with me, Michael. At the back of the bus, where Mervyn and I were sitting. I have kept the place with my jacket.' It was an order, not an invitation. He turned: 'Mervyn will sit with Jutta.'

No doubt I should have said: 'Perhaps Jutta would like to sit with you.' But such self-sacrifice was beyond me.

Jürgen strode down the aisle ahead of me to the back of the charabanc, and edged himself into the seat in the corner. Then he patted the seat next to it: 'Michael! Michael! Come!'

Across the aisle in the back row, two Germans, a boy and girl, had already resumed their former seats.

Mervyn hesitated by the seats in front of Jürgen's and mine. 'Would you like to sit by the window, Jutta? You'll be able to see better.'

'There is nothing to see,' she replied in the pinched, woeful voice of an overtired child. 'You sit there. I think it will rain soon,' she added.

Far off thunder crackled. Mervyn listened to it, head

171

on one side. He pulled a face. 'You may be right.' Then he flopped down in the seat by the window.

Jutta placed herself beside him with a sigh. '*Ach*, I am tired!' Her hands busied themselves at the ribbons with which she had tied her hair into short, outsticking braids. In those braids, ankle socks and low-heeled strap shoes, she looked – as she'd looked when I'd first set eyes on her, so long ago it now seemed – like a small girl.

'You don't have to bother about talking to me,' Mervyn said. 'I'm tired too. We both can have a zizz.'

'Zizz?'

'A sleep.'

'Yes, let us have a zizz, Mervyn.'

Jeremy, having overheard the conversation, turned round grinning. 'Yes, go to sleep, both of you. Then I can tell everyone that Mervyn and Jutta slept together on the bus.'

Playfully, Jutta half rose, leaned forward, raised her handbag and hit him with it across the head. 'Jeremy, you are a terrible boy.'

At last the bus, held up by a German girl who had left her rucksack behind in the café, set off. As the sun began to disappear behind the livid clouds, some of the German students began to bawl out folk-songs with a lot of jolly 'Hee-hee-hee' and 'Ho-ho-ho.' Then they called on the English students for a folk song.

'Oh, God! Now what shall we do?' Harry lurched up, with one foot in the aisle and the other resting on the seat that he'd just vacated. He shouted to the English: 'What about "There is a Tavern in the Town"?'

'Oh, no! ... Too corny! ... For heaven's sake!' The English voices jangled and jarred. I wished that they'd all shut up.

Jeremy now also stood up in the aisle. 'We could always

172

give them "It was the Good Ship Venus". That would make them sit up.'

'Oh, Jeremy!' Jessica exclaimed, disgusted.

'Sit down, Jeremy!' Harry shouted at him.

But undaunted, Jeremy began to sing. No one joined in or paid him any attention. Then Edna leaned forward and tugged at his shirt. 'Stop it! That's enough!' With a self-congratulatory laugh, as though he'd performed some difficult feat, Jeremy bounced back into his seat.

From time to time the bus would jolt and shudder over some obstruction in the road. Each time that it did so, at least one of the girls would let out a squeal. Then even that ceased. Everyone was drowsy, if not already drowsing. I could see Mervyn's face reflected in the window, the eyes shut. For once he looked young, puzzled, vulnerable. Touched by a pathos previously unrevealed to me, I felt an impulse of tenderness rare in our matter-of-fact, often comradely, sometimes contentious, relationship. Jutta's head slipped sideways. She steadied it, straightened, gave a little cough. Then, a minute later, her head again slipped sideways, this time coming to rest on Mervyn's shoulder. He shifted and made a small grimace in his sleep, as though the contact irked him. Then he once again relapsed into immobility.

Jürgen shifted, thrusting out his long, sunburned legs in those shorts so much shorter than any worn by the English, so that he inadvertently kicked the back of the seats in which Jutta and Mervyn were asleep. But he did not wake them. Leaning sideways against the window, down which rain had now become a trickle, he raised an arm and placed it about my shoulders.

At the touch of his bare arm on the bare flesh of my neck above my shirt, my whole body shuddered, as though at a gust of icy air in a previously heated room. A sigh trembled from me. Now his hand fell, as though

173

naturally in that posture, on to my thigh. He turned to me, smiling. He brought his lips near. Tantalisingly, he looked into my eyes for seconds on end before at last, at long last, his lips closed on mine. Panic-stricken, I looked across the aisle. But the two Germans were as deeply asleep as Jutta and Mervyn.

What Jürgen did next astonished, terrified and thrilled me. Slowly, button by button, he undid the fly of his shorts, his lower lip caught between his teeth with the effort in that cramped space. Then he reached into the shorts to bring out his penis, so swollen that the veins stood out on it like cords. He took my hand in his, and placed it on the penis, the tip already tacky. It throbbed at my touch. I wanted to cry out 'Stop it! Not here! No!' I wanted to push his hand from me and to snatch away my own hand, against which the penis, hard and rampant, was pushing. But I could not do so.

Then his hand was on the back of my head. Inexorably it pressed my head downwards, downwards, downwards, towards the crotch revealed by the gaping shorts.

XVI

When the charabanc arrived at the university square, Jürgen leapt up from his seat, pushed past me without a word, and rushed the length of the bus to jump off it before anyone else.

Mervyn, still slit-eyed from sleep, raised a hand to his mouth and yawned luxuriously behind it. 'Where's he rushing to?'

'I think he must pay the charas,' Jutta said, reaching up for her rucksack. Whereas sleep had made Mervyn look even more tired, it had revived her. 'He has the money. He must pay the driver in the front chara.' Each time that she said the word 'chara', she did so with obvious pleasure.

'Well, that was fun,' Edna remarked in a tone of voice that suggested that she wasn't really sure if it had been fun or not. Then she peered over at me, her eyes narrowing. 'All right?'

'Yes, of course. Why?'

'You look so pale.'

'I expect Michael is tired,' Jutta said, staring at me with the same intentness.

'Yes, I am tired,' I said, both embarrassed and cross. 'And I feel bus-sick.'

'But on the boat you were one of the few people who didn't succumb,' Jeremy reminded me.

'It's so stuffy in here. It was a question of either opening the window and letting in the rain, or keeping it shut and suffocating.'

Jeremy reached up for his bag. Glasses clinked as he

lifted it down. 'Yes, it *is* stuffy. Why the hell don't people move?'

But a shuffle towards the door had already begun.

'So what's the plan now?' I asked Mervyn. I longed to be with Jürgen, and yet shrank in shame and embarrassment from another encounter.

'Well, I've Heinrich's parents coming, as you know. I'll have to give them dinner. You're coming along to help me out, aren't you? And you, Jutta?'

'Thank you.' Jutta's voice was again the listless, forlorn one of an overtired little girl. As at the picnic, I wondered how much she'd seen and how much she'd guessed. But she couldn't have seen anything – how could she? – seated as she'd been in front of us, with her head on Mervyn's shoulder and her eyes shut. 'What time do you want me?'

'In half an hour? They'll have already arrived at the house, I'm afraid. I'd no idea the journey would take so long and we'd get back so late. I suppose the Prof and the sisters are entertaining them. I certainly hope they are.

'I will wash and change. I will see if Sally is all right. Then I will walk over. Yes?'

When we'd at last got off the bus, I looked for Jürgen, my eyes going frantically from one group of people to another. But I couldn't see him anywhere.

'No sign of Jürgen,' I said at last, in what I hoped was a matter-of-fact voice.

'No sign of Jürgen,' Mervyn echoed. Was he mocking me?

'Perhaps he must go to the office of the chara company in order to pay.' Jutta then turned to ask Jo, who was standing near us with a group of his friends, if he knew where Jürgen was.

Jo shrugged. 'You know Jürgen. We all know Jürgen.'

'Oh, there's Duffy!' Edna cried out. 'What an angel!

176

He must have guessed how tired I'd be after all that walking.'

In a dark-blue polo-neck sweater, grey flannels and sandals which displayed toenails the colour and consistency of cow-horn, Duffy bustled over. 'Well, how went the expedition?'

'Why didn't you warn us about Rosenheim?' I asked.

'Is *that* where you went? They told me they were planning to take you to the lake. Lovely place – walks, sailing, swimming. Well, well! The artful beggars! No wonder you all look so depressed. Rosenheim could hardly be called *fun*. It's one of those *once* places that now exist all over this bloody country. You know, when people talk about it, they always begin "Once ..."' He turned to Edna: 'Well, shall we get cracking?'

Edna looked at Jutta and me. 'I know it's a little out of your way, Duffy dear, but do you think you could bear to give Jutta and Michael a lift to their lodgings?'

'Of course! Glad to! No sweat!'

'And perhaps you could very kindly drop me off too,' Jeremy put in.

'Oh, Jeremy, you can *walk*!' Edna told him crossly. 'It's no distance at all, only ten minutes or so. You know it's right out of the way, and that it's always difficult for three people in the back of that car – particularly with all these things.'

'All right, all right,' Jeremy said in a sulky, disappointed voice, turning away from us.

'Look, old chap – ' Duffy began. But Edna interrupted: 'Oh, let him walk, Duffy. It'll be good for him.'

Jeremy slunk off, with no further word or even glance in our direction.

XVII

I rushed up to my room, threw off all my clothes, splashed some water out of the ewer into the washbasin, and hurriedly washed myself all over. From the bed the dog watched me with eyes misty with cataracts. Then, overcome by an irresistible lassitude, I fell across the bed, so close to the dog that my nostrils filled with the musty odour, by no means disagreeable, that emanated from her fur, and at once fell asleep.

Some twenty minutes later I awoke. Christ, Mervyn was expecting me! Having thrown on a clean shirt, a tie and another pair of trousers, I hurried over to the house.

Surprisingly it was not Jürgen or some other member of his family who answered the bell, but Mervyn.

'Have they arrived?'

'I'm afraid so. The Prof and Hilde have gone out to a concert, so Marthe has been helping me to entertain them.' He leaned forward to whisper: 'The mother looks like a retired tart. Not at all what I'd expected. And he's not Heinrich's father but his stepfather. The father was killed by a bomb in the first two weeks of the war. Why did Heinrich never tell us?'

At that moment Jutta appeared, crying out 'Sorry, sorry – I am bad girl – I am late!' as she hurried up the drive.

In the drawing-room the two visitors sat on the high-backed, lumpy sofa, each grasping a small glass of some kind of ruby liqueur. Marthe sat opposite to them, her knitting clicking away under her small, wobbly chin, as she conversed in a softly pattering German. There was no sign of Jürgen. What had become of him?

Mervyn's comment that Heinrich's mother looked like a retired tart had been cruel. But, with too much lipstick on her mouth, smeared carelessly upwards at one corner, eyes circled with purple eye-shadow, and innumerable rings biting deep into her fingers, she certainly gave an impression of soiled, provocative blowsiness.

Her husband was small, grey-faced, grey-haired, with knobbly hands that had clearly been scrubbed vigorously to remove the stains that could be seen in the crevices around his finger-nails. Later, he was to reveal that he was a shoemaker. How had two such totally different people ever come together?

Having greeted Jutta and me, Marthe crossed over to the piano and poured us out some of the sticky, sweet liqueur – it could only be home-made, I decided when I'd tasted it. She'd not enquired whether we wanted it or not. Each time that she extended the glasses, she gave a funny little bobbing curtsey and murmured '*Bitte.*'

'No Jürgen?' I said to Mervyn, telling myself that he was probably still having a bath or shower and changing, but not really believing it.

'I'm afraid not. Apparently he got a message from his professor to go round and see him. Or, at least, that's what he said. It's not the first time he's made that excuse, is it? One can only assume that the professor must have a crush on him.' Was he deliberately trying to upset me?

'Isn't he going to join us later?'

He shrugged. 'He said he'd try. After all, it *is* our last night.'

I knew, even then, that he would not join us. With that realisation came an intense desire to get up, excuse myself and return to my room. But, unless I pretended to feel ill, how could I do that? Mervyn would never forgive me. After all, Heinrich was also a friend of mine.

The others began to talk again in German. Motionless, the glass untouched in my hand, I looked in turn into their faces, in an attempt to guess what each of them was saying. From time to time Mervyn would give me a summary, but in a manner so off-hand, even impatient, that it was all too clear that to do so was a nuisance for him. Frau Hartmann was leaning forward, her pudgy hands, with their chipped crimson nail-varnish, clasped tight before her and her face haggard with passion, as though she were begging this English visitor to save her son's life. She constantly asked rushed, nervous questions, to which Mervyn would first give some weary answer, and then provide me with a no less weary translation of what had been said. Inevitably, what Frau Hartmann was most eager to learn about was the conditions in which her son lived. Did he have enough to eat? Was his hut very cold? Was the road-work that he did on the bypass between Oxford and Woodstock very hard?

Through all this her husband sat stiff and silent. His glass was long since empty but he still held it, two knobbly fingers around the bowl and two around the spindly stem, high up against his chest, as though about to propose a toast. Once, his pale-blue eyes, under eyebrows so faint that they were almost imperceptible, met mine, and he then gave me a small, furtive, apologetic smile.

The knitting-needles clicked away. At one moment, Jutta leaned forward and stroked what was clearly going to be one of the sleeves of Jürgen's pullover. Marthe looked up and murmured something, in which I heard Jürgen's name twice, and the two women then laughed delightedly.

Eventually we set off for the restaurant, through the thick, heavy air that the brief storm had been insufficient to clear. Frau Hartmann slipped an arm through her husband's. Mervyn walked beside them, leaving Jutta and me to follow. He'd invited Marthe to come too, but she'd treated the invitation as a joke, throwing back her head and laughing. She rarely went out, she explained. She must now prepare a meal for her sister and brother.

The food in the restaurant was even more disgusting than on previous occasions when we'd eaten here. There was a soup, consisting of cauliflower, lumps of potato and a few coarse slivers of mutton, with iridescent patches of fat floating on its surface. Herr Hartmann began to dunk pieces of his 'utility bread' in it until a frown from his wife stopped him in embarrassment. Mervyn had translated the next course as liver, but it seemed to me more likely that the grey, spongy lumps, masked in a red-wine sauce, were the lung or spleen that, back home in England, we fed to the cat. The Hartmanns devoured this dish as voraciously as they'd devoured their soup and bread. So did Jutta, her expression frowningly intent, as though over some difficult task. It was odd to be served food so repellent on a spotless white damask cloth, and to eat it off delicate china, its scalloped edges picked out in gold.

Frau Hartmann continued to ask her rushed, anxious questions. At one point her eyes filled with tears, which then blurred her mascara, so that she looked even more pathetic and grotesque. Her husband extended a hand and put it over hers. But she clearly did not care for this contact, withdrawing her hand from under his and slipping it into her lap.

Jutta leaned across the table to me. 'Mervyn has been good to this Heinrich.'

'Yes, he's been good to him.'

'Mervyn is a good man.' Jutta said it with conviction.

It was something that had never occurred to me. An intelligent man, a witty man, a cultivated man, an entertaining man: yes, he was all of those things. But a *good* man?

Later, Jutta said: 'I do not think that Jürgen will join us now.'

I stared down at the glare of the damask table-cloth under a light unusually bright for the town. 'I never thought he would.'

Mervyn, overhearing us, broke off his conversation with the Hartmanns. 'Neither did I. If there's one thing that Jürgen abominates, it's to be bored.'

I gulped at my hock. I knew that, if I were not careful, I'd soon be drunk. But I wanted to be drunk, even if it disgraced me.

At long last the Hartmanns said they must go to the railway station. They'd had a long journey, all the way from Dusseldorf, and now they had a long journey back again. Mervyn was surprised. I guessed that he was now asking them why they were not spending the night in Hildingen before setting off for home. Herr Hartmann made a gesture of rubbing finger and thumb together: it was a question of money, that universal gesture indicated. He arose and then stooped for the two bags which he'd refused to allow a supercilious young waiter with heavily pomaded hair to take from him on our entry. The bags contained the presents from Heinrich and Mervyn.

Frau Hartmann, still slumped mournfully in her chair, mascara streaked round her eyes and lipstick streaked round one corner of her mouth, opened the huge handbag, its leather the colour and texture of elephant hide, which she'd placed on the floor beside her surprisingly small feet. She took out a package wrapped in tissue paper, and handed it to me with a smile.

'What is it?'

Frau Hartmann said something and Mervyn then

182

translated: 'She says open it and see. It's something not for you but for your mother.'

I wanted to say: But she's never met my mother. But instead I began to peel off the tissue paper.

Inside, there were three handkerchiefs of a lawn so fine that it was almost transparent. Each was beautifully embroidered in one corner with an edelweiss in coloured silk.

'Did she work this?'

Frau Hartmann looked apologetic as she gave her answer. No, the embroidery had been done by one of her aunts.

I felt embarrassed at having myself brought no present for the Hartmanns. 'Tell them that, when I get back to England, I'll send them a food-parcel.'

When Mervyn had translated this, both Hartmanns shook their heads vigorously and began to protest. But their sudden jollity betrayed their true response.

At his wife's bidding – imperiously she pointed – Herr Hartmann now again stooped to retrieve from the floor a flat, square parcel in brown paper, which he'd carried under one arm on the way to the restaurant. He bowed as he held this parcel out to Mervyn.

I could guess that Mervyn was asking 'Is this for me?', in the ungracious tone which he always adopted when given a present, and that, as he then mumbled his thanks, the Hartmanns were urging him to see what it was. Probably because he was thinking of all the bother of rewrapping the parcel, Mervyn was unwilling to comply, so that it was Jutta who eventually took it from him, untied the string and pulled off the paper. She looked down at the object revealed, her face transfigured. Then, triumphantly, she held it up for all of us to see.

It was a sampler, meticulously worked in cross-stitch, of a square house, with smoke wreathing out from its chimney, and, in the foreground, a bed of hollyhocks, with a woman, dressed in a billowing purple crinoline and poke-bonnet, standing under a parasol, with a pug dog beside her. Jutta lowered the sampler in its heavily ornate gilt frame and, staring down at it again, said all the complimentary things that Mervyn should have been saying.

'And did her aunt work that too?'

Jutta put my question to Frau Hartmann, who burst into laughter before she answered.

'No, not her aunt,' Jutta translated. 'Her grandmother.'

'So it's old?'

Jutta also put this question to Frau Hartmann, who nodded.

'Very, very old.'

'Oh, you shouldn't take it, Mervyn. It's, well, an heirloom isn't it?'

'I don't *want* to take it. It's the last thing I want. But I think I'll have to.'

The Hartmanns were gazing at him, nodding their heads, in indulgent happiness. As ungraciously as before, he repeated his thanks.

Outside the restaurant, suddenly saddened by the fate of this large, overpainted woman bereft of her only son, I suggested 'Let's walk them to the station.'

'Oh, God no! I've had quite enough walking for one day, thank you.'

When we said our goodbyes, Frau Hartmann grasped my right hand in both of hers and, looking searchingly into my face, said something insistent in German.

I turned to Jutta, not Mervyn. 'What is she saying?'

'She is saying that you are a very charming young man. Very handsome. She is saying that she hopes that you will come again to Germany.' Frau Hartmann added something further, still clutching my hand, and Jutta then continued: 'She says that her son is lucky to know you. She says that she wishes you to have a happy journey. She says that she greets your parents.' As each of these sentiments was relayed to me, I gave a small, embarrassed smile and a nod.

Herr Hartmann was far more restrained, merely taking my hand in his rough one and muttering goodbye.

Frau Hartmann now went over to Mervyn, who visibly shrank away from her. With a choking sob, she threw a plump arm round his neck and pulled his head down towards her. She kissed him on first one cheek and then the other. Over her shoulder, Mervyn's eyes were panicky. It seemed to me that vicariously the German woman was embracing Heinrich through this aloof, embarrassed English friend of his. '*Ach!*' She pulled a handkerchief from the belt of her dress, and held it first to one eye and then the other.

We stood close together in the dim circle of light shed by the lamp-post outside the restaurant and watched as the Hartmanns – oddly distanced from each other, he with the parcels dangling one from each hand, she with her head thrown back as though in defiance of some invisible assailant ahead – moved off into the darkness.

'What an evening!' Mervyn exclaimed.

'They are so sweet,' Jutta said. 'And so sad.'

The Hartmanns turned as they reached the place where the road made a crook to the left of the Town Hall. She raised a hand and waved, and Jutta and I then waved back at her. Mervyn, standing stiffly to attention, did not do so.

'What an evening!' he repeated. Then he said: 'Let's walk Jutta home.'

Jutta protested – it was late, we were tired, she often walked home alone – but we would have none of it.

185

At the door of her lodging-house, Jutta looked at me and said: 'I am sorry that Jürgen did not come.'

'Yes.' I was guarded. 'He'd have made the evening more entertaining, wouldn't he?'

'Oh, but I enjoyed!' Jutta said.

I almost again told her, as Mervyn and I had so often told her in the past, that 'enjoy' was a transitive, not an intransitive, verb. But I felt too tired and depressed, I could not be bothered.

She placed her latch-key in the door, hesitated and then looked back. 'Jürgen will come to see you off. You will see him tomorrow.' She turned the latch-key.

'Yes – if his professor doesn't want to see him again,' I all but answered out of the bitterness welling up in me like a brackish spring. Then I decided to say nothing. Perhaps by now he'd returned from his visit to his professor – if, indeed, he'd ever made it – and I should see him at the house.

Mervyn and I were silent as we made our way down the already deserted main road and then along a lane winding between mean, red-brick houses that might have been part of a council estate anywhere in England. At one moment a dog barked hysterically from behind a wall at the sound of our footsteps. At another moment we passed an ancient drunk, his hat tipped over his eyes, who was weaving along the path, singing softly to himself. He gave us a hoarse '*Gute Nacht! Gute Nacht!* as he stood back for us. Mervyn replied with a shouted '*Gute Nacht!*' over his shoulder.

I walked with Mervyn up to the front-door of the house. He craned his head upwards. All the windows were dark, with the exception of the hall one. 'Too late to ask you in. Clearly everyone's gone to bed.'

'D'you think Jürgen's back?' I couldn't stop myself from putting the question.

'Who knows?' Mervyn said.

I wanted to say: 'Let's go in and see,' but restrained myself, with a feeling of despairing impotence.

'I expect he's out on another of his shagging expeditions. I just hope he doesn't make too much noise when he comes up.'

XVIII

Although it was before seven o'clock, most of the Germans had turned up to say goodbye to us in the university square. Two of the three buses of the day before, with the same military-looking drivers, stood parked behind one another, with Hanover, not Rosenheim, displayed in front as their destination.

Jutta had insisted on carrying Sally's suitcase, jogging along with it, since we were late, in such a lopsided manner, the muscles in her thin legs straining, that she looked as if at any moment she would topple over. 'Oh, do let me carry that!' Sally kept protesting. But Jutta'd have none of it, vigorously shaking her head, mouth screwed up and eyes narrowed in concentration, as she hurried on down the hill.

'It's going to be another scorcher,' I said, hurrying behind her with my own suitcase.

'Scorcher?'

'Very hot.'

'*Ja* – scorcher!' Like 'nightcap' and 'chara', 'scorcher' would clearly now become part of Jutta's English vocabulary.

Barely acknowledging the students, English and German, who greeted us, Jutta hobbled over to the first of the two buses and began to shove the suitcase into its open baggage hold. I then pushed in mine. 'Sally! Sally!' Jutta shouted, seeing that Sally'd been waylaid by a group of Germans, all of whom seemed to be in as much of a state of excitement as we who were leaving. 'Bring your rucksack here. I will put it away for you.'

Although Jutta tried to seize the rucksack, it was I who relieved Sally of it and pushed it into the hold. Jutta's face and bare arms were glistening with sweat. 'Oh, Jutta,' Sally cried out, 'you should have let me carry the case at least part of the way. Look how hot you are!'

'You are the guest.'

'Well ... ' Sally smiled. Then, with one of those spontaneous gestures of hers, which still have the power to touch me, she suddenly put up a hand to Jutta's shiny cheek and tenderly let it rest there. 'I hope that one day *you*'ll be *my* guest. You have my address? Write to me, Jutta. And try to come to stay when it's possible for you to do so. Promise?'

Jutta made no promise. 'You are very kind,' she said in a grave troubled voice.

I looked about me, screwing up my eyes as I faced into the sun still low over the grey-tiled roof of the Aula. A hand waved and then a voice shouted: 'Michael! Sally!' It was Jeremy, jumping up and down in a knot of the English in order to attract our notice. He might have been a young boy about to leave his prep-school for the summer holidays.

'What's happened to Mervyn?' Sally said. 'Fancy oversleeping, today of all days! If he doesn't come soon, he's going to miss the bus.'

'Surely the bus will not go without him,' Jutta said.

'It certainly will – if the alternative is for all of us to miss our train.'

'This is a sad, sad moment.' Thwaites's hand was on my shoulder, his body so close to mine that I could feel the roughness of his tweed jacket on my bare arm. 'I got up at six o'clock this morning so that I could see you all off. And of course bring our Edna down.' He sighed, drawing down the corners of his mouth. 'I'll miss the dear girl – for all her naughtinesses.'

I gave him a perfunctory smile. 'I can't see Mervyn.' What I really meant was: I can't see Jürgen.

'Isn't he on the other side of the bus? I rather think I saw him there.'

'Oh, is he?'

Leaving Thwaites, I hurried round the bus. Mervyn was indeed there, exchanging addresses with a small group of Germans. 'Oh, there you are, Mervyn! Thank goodness! Sally and I were afraid you'd miss the bus.'

'Is that likely? Anyway, you were supposed to keep it for me.'

'Isn't Jürgen with you?'

'Jürgen? Nope. As I told you, he never came home last night. But I had a word with him. Telephoned.'

'Telephoned! He telephoned? But you never told me that.' I felt sure that he had deliberately withheld this information from me.

'Oh, I was in such a rush – oversleeping like that. He said something about missing the last bus and staying the night at the professor's. I don't believe it for a moment – unless the professor is both female and young. You know our Jürgen.'

I said nothing. I felt a terrible desolation.

'He asked me to bid you a fond farewell. At least, I think it was fond.' There was something of the dryness and harshness of sandpaper in the way in which he said the last sentence. Yes, yes, I decided, he knew what had happened between Jürgen and me. And he knew what I was suffering.

I stood behind the bus, hoping that no one would speak to me before its departure. But inevitably that hope was vain. German after German sought me out, to wish me a happy journey, to exchange addresses, even to give me some present – which Jutta, who had joined me, would then officiously take from me and put in a basket.

Where she'd found this basket, I couldn't imagine.

At last the driver of the first of the two buses blew energetically on a whistle and began shouting in German. Everyone yet again said goodbye.

'Ah, Michael, Michael!' Jutta threw her arms about me and hugged me to her. Her lower lip was trembling.

With a sudden, violent upsurge of emotion, which took me wholly by surprise, I in turn threw my arms around her and kissed her on the lips. 'Goodbye, Jutta. Thank you, thank you! And – good luck!'

'Good luck, Michael.' Jutta screwed up her face, as though she were about to cry.

On the bus, Mervyn and I sat side by side on the same seats on which Jürgen and I had sat on the return from Rosenheim the previous evening. Sally sat across the aisle. She looked strangely troubled and sad.

'Well!' Mervyn took a dirty, rumpled handkerchief out of his grey flannel slacks and first mopped at his forehead and then wiped the palms of his hands. 'So that's that.' He said it without regret. 'Tomorrow we'll be back in dear, run-down, muddled old England.'

I gazed out of the window at the brown fields stretching on and on, level to the horizon. I made no answer.

Mervyn turned his head and stared at me. 'Cheer up! Surely you're not depressed at leaving this ghastly country?' I realised that I must be looking as Sally was.

'I don't know. I don't know what I feel.'

'You rarely do, do you?' Then he laughed, as though to demonstrate that he intended no malice.

'Where's your present?' I suddenly asked. 'You didn't put it with the other luggage, did you? The glass might get broken.'

'What present?'

'The sampler.'

'Oh, I couldn't be bothered to lug something so hideous halfway across Europe! I gave it to Marthe. She kept clucking "*Schön, schön, schön!*" when I showed it to her over breakfast, so I thought, Well, let her have it, very much to her taste.'

'Oh, Mervyn, how could you, how *could* you?'

'Would you have liked it?'

'No, of course not, but ... what are you going to say to Heinrich?'

'Why should I say anything to him?'

'Well, isn't his mother going to tell him she gave it to you? And isn't he then going to look for it and ask to see it, when next you have him round?'

'Oh, Christ!' Mervyn slapped his forehead. 'I hadn't thought of that. Well, I'll just have to say someone stole it on the journey home. At the docks at the Hook. Why not? Things get stolen when one travels. And *what* would be more likely to get stolen than a beautiful sampler of a woman in a crinoline and poke bonnet?' He grinned at me.

I closed my eyes. I wanted to sleep. I wanted to dream. I wanted to remember. I wanted to escape from Mervyn's sarcasm, from the rowdy voices around me. Above all, I wanted once again to be with Jürgen.

XIX

In the first weeks which followed our return, I wrote Jürgen many letters. But unlike the letters written to other Germans in Hildingen – written, I realise now, with no purpose other than to get news of him – those letters had no answer.

When Sally and I sent him an invitation to our wedding – oddly, it was she who suggested that we do so, although she didn't suggest that we should also send one to Jutta – that, too, received no answer.

Two or three years later, a Christmas card arrived for Sally, not me. Mysteriously, it was addressed to her by her maiden name, at her family's home in York. 'We'd better send one back,' Sally said. The next year we again sent a card. But no other card ever came.

The last time that Sally spoke to me of Jürgen was when, pensively nursing our first child by the fire one winter, she suddenly remarked, apropos of nothing, 'I wonder what became of Jürgen.'

'Yes, I wonder.' It was something that I'd often and often wondered, although I'd never told her so.

'He wanted to be an actor, didn't he? But if he'd had any success, we'd have heard of it.'

'Would we?'

'Well, if he'd had any success in films.' She stared out of the window at the snow thick in the branches of the sycamore beneath which I'm sitting on this early morning of summer. 'He looked on us as punishers.'

'Only at first.'

'And so he wanted to punish us in return.'

'That was Mervyn's idea.'

'Mine too. One of the best ways to punish people is to show them what they are.'

What did she mean? Could she mean what I thought she meant? 'It was a difficult time.'

'A terrible time.'

There was a silence. Then: 'Perhaps he's dead.'

'Perhaps,' I answered.

But he could not be dead! No one so vivid in my secret, guilty life of memory and fantasy could possibly be dead. If he were dead, I should know.

A few years ago, I was in Hamburg for a medical conference. Late one night, lonely and drunk, I picked up the phone and dialled the number which I'd copied, in an obstinate act of faith, through a succession of address books over a succession of years. But all I heard in response was a high-pitched whine, as though those Hildingen gnats were again tormenting me by the river. I dialled again and again. Eventually I asked the operator for her help. 'No such number, sir,' she said. The name 'Koesten' did not even appear in the Hildingen directory.

Again I dialled the number in my diary. Then, naked, I lay across the bed, the receiver pressed to my ear, as on and on that gnat whine, shrill and unrelenting, sounded through the dry, disintegrating husk that I seemed to have become.

1981

There is a wood, like the woods around Hildingen through which we would walk. There is a straight, dusty road, with hedgerows on either side, so high that it is impossible to see over them. Jutta and Sally and Mervyn and Edna and Jeremy and all the other students are walking up the road ahead of me. They are contented enough, chattering to each other, laughing together, even indulging in horseplay. But I do not want to join them. I am happy to trail behind.

All at once I come on a place, little more than a hole in the hedgerow, where a narrow, overgrown path zigzags off into the undergrowth. Jürgen is standing at the entrance to the hole. Sometimes he is in a khaki shirt and khaki trousers. More often he is stripped to the waist and wearing only those shortest of shorts. He beckons to me. Smiles. Beckons again. But I shake my head violently. I hurry on. I hurry on after the others, drawing breath on breath with an increasingly painful effort. Then I hear him laughing – no, not mockingly but joyfully – no, not at me but at something in himself ...

That is the dream, the second dream. The first dream is of that journey by bus. From time to time I dream this second dream. I have just dreamed it here, dozing in this garden chair, with the cat on my lap. *The other path.* I call it the dream of the other path.

Disturbing my memory of the dream, Sally is coming down the garden, over the dewy lawn towards me, a glass in either hand. Her silk kimono, bought on our visit last year to Japan, is flecked with the light that falls through the branches. It might be flecked with sequins. Her hair, now greying, is in a long plait down her back. I've got used to that plait, I no longer hate it, as once I used to do. In the glasses is the juice of the oranges that she has squeezed with her strong, competent hands in the kitchen. She holds out a glass.

'First course,' she says. 'I'll fry the eggs and bacon in a minute.'

As I take the glass from her, the cat, capricious as always, leaps off my lap, whisks into the herbaceous border, and is lost to view.

Sally raises her glass. The sunlight, glinting on it, makes it look as if it were foaming with blood.

We bring our glasses together and then simultaneously sip, as though partaking of a sacrament of a religion in which I can never do more than pretend – and yes, try, try so agonisingly, try so futilely – to share her belief.